That much Eve was sure of. She fought off a rising sense of panic, and tried to order her thoughts. No, she was in a parking lot, filled, as if this were an ordinary workday.

It must have been the fall she'd taken. Had it caused her to lose some days? That was scary, but she could live with that, she decided, taking a deep breath and closing her eyes. Instantly, a vision of herself in Sam's arms, his mouth tenderly closing on hers, assailed her. She could once again feel him, taste him, smell him....

No! That couldn't have happened. It went against everything she knew about Sam—and herself.

"I must have imagined that kiss because of the blow to my head," she told herself forcefully.

But nothing imagined had ever felt so good....

ACKNOWLEDGMENTS

Research is always fun, and these wonderful people gave me information about:

Mary Bothwell—Australia

Dr. Henry Downs—Head injuries

Dr. Gloria Houston—Civilian Employment in the U.S. Navy (my first piano teacher)

Nancy Ryanen-Grant—Computer Security

Craig Scammell—Australia

Richard Schettler—Careers in the U.S. Navy

Sharon at the Chamber of Commerce— Pacific Grove, CA

Pam Tanous, Chamber of Commerce—Monterey, CA

Gwyn Weathers, Monterey Foreign Language Institute—Monterey, CA

AOL and Prodigy surfers—Particle Physics and Church Services

Phyllis Houseman

ANOTHER NEW YEAR'S EVE

Harlequin Books

TORONTO • NEW YORK • LONDON
AMSTERDAM • PARIS • SYDNEY • HAMBURG
STOCKHOLM • ATHENS • TOKYO • MILAN
MADRID • WARSAW • BUDAPEST • AUCKLAND

In loving memory of my mother, Sylvia Greenberg, who always had time for her daughters, and taught them the fine art of making potato *latkes*.
To Jack—for catching all those sinking canoe paddles, and for your love.
To Valerie and Daniel—Our wonderful children. I'm so proud of you both.

ISBN 0-373-16659-1

ANOTHER NEW YEAR'S EVE

Copyright © 1996 by Phyllis Houseman.

All rights reserved. Except for use in any review, the reproduction or utilization of this work in whole or in part in any form by any electronic, mechanical or other means, now known or hereafter invented, including xerography, photocopying and recording, or in any information storage or retrieval system, is forbidden without the written permission of the publisher, Harlequin Enterprises Limited, 225 Duncan Mill Road, Don Mills, Ontario, Canada M3B 3K9.

All characters in this book have no existence outside the imagination of the author and have no relation whatsoever to anyone bearing the same name or names. They are not even distantly inspired by any individual known or unknown to the author, and all incidents are pure invention.

This edition published by arrangement with Harlequin Books S.A.

® and TM are trademarks of the publisher. Trademarks indicated with ® are registered in the United States Patent and Trademark Office, the Canadian Trade Marks Office and in other countries.

Printed in U.S.A.

Prologue

"Mozart's in the closet. Let him out, let him out, let him out!"

Eve Gray pulled into the supermarket parking space just as the radio trumpeted the opening bars of Mozart's fortieth symphony. When the music began, the insidious lyric burst from her mouth before she knew it, exploding into the mild Monterey night through the open driver's side window of her little gold Toyota.

She turned off her car and its radio with a quick twist of the ignition key. Eve's green eyes anxiously scanned the nearly deserted area. She hoped no one had heard her infectious little performance.

But, of course, there *would* be a man sitting in the dark blue station wagon to her left. And on a November night that was unusually warm, even for California, his windows were also wide open.

It was then Eve realized that the Mozart symphony played on in the quiet Safeway parking lot.

But even as she peered into the neighboring vehicle, the dark-haired driver inside switched off the classical radio station and directed a smile at her.

It was only a quick, friendly grin, but for a significant interval of time, Eve forgot to breathe. Gorgeous . . . absolutely gorgeous! Even if she didn't have a photographic memory, his was a face she would never forget.

White, white teeth were set in a wide, sensual mouth. Thick, dark hair fell over a high, square forehead. She couldn't tell the color of his eyes, but they gleamed with mischief and somehow seemed a perfect complement to his cute snub nose, which hinted at an Irish ancestry.

Shaken by the impact the whole package of features made on her, Eve could only sit and watch while automatic windows closed and the man exited his car. Very tall and broad-chested, he strode toward the nearby grocery entrance.

"Mozart's in the closet. Let him out, let him out, let—"

The store's electric doors slid shut, cutting off the man's pleasant baritone voice and the rest of the dreaded verse.

"Oh, no," Eve groaned out loud. "I've doomed another poor soul!" He'd find out that, like a virus, the silly ditty had lodged in his brain, where it would taint the wonderful piece of music forevermore.

She had been contaminated by it three years ago in a college music history class. No doubt the professor only thought he was giving his students a way to remember the piece among the dozens they needed to identify during exams. And it had worked. Oh, how well it had worked!

Locking up her car, Eve straightened her business suit and then rushed into the store. She had an almost irresistible urge to follow the man strolling down the dairy aisle and apologize. *Of course, the impulse has absolutely nothing to do with his face and body,* Eve's conscience taunted.

Well, it was not that she needed to resort to grocery-store pickups. Lots of eligible men around the government facility where she worked asked her out, and she accepted their invitations as often as she wanted.

Only, I haven't felt much like starting the dating game again, she thought, unconsciously rubbing the bare ring finger of her left hand where the diamond had been.

Almost against her will, Eve's eyes followed the stranger, who was tossing item after item into his cart. *Funny, he isn't even my type... blond and blue-eyed.*

Yet, there she stood, her body poised over her basket, high-heeled shoes ready to push off after the man.

No. No matter how sexy his smile, or how tempting meeting him might be, she was not about to waylay the guy between the domestic cheese and yogurt displays!

Going to the right instead of the left, she resolutely pushed her cart through the almost deserted store, turning down the baking products aisle that held most of the things she needed.

"Hi, Maria," Eve greeted the checker a few minutes later. "How are your husband and little *niña* doing?"

"Eve, how nice to see you. Don't tell me you're just getting off work! It's after eleven," the dark-eyed young woman chided as she surveyed Eve's outfit and then positioned the cart nearer to the conveyer belt.

Yawning, Eve smiled at Maria Hidalgo, touched by her concern. It *was* late. And this was only Tuesday. The pretest countdown procedures for Project LinkUp were generating a ton of data she would need to analyze in the coming days. The full-scale test wasn't scheduled until New Year's Eve—at the stroke of midnight, in fact. But there would be a lot of late nights before the actual trial run in four weeks' time.

"You're right, I did work late. I had to verify some...details," Eve carefully acknowledged. She always kept the need for security in mind when talking to anybody without the proper clearances.

"I can't believe it's almost two months since my sister's wedding," Maria commented. "Everybody still talks about your piano playing. It made the ceremony so lovely. But to get back to your questions, my husband is fine—Roberto's doing well at his new job, *gracias a Dios*—and the *niña* isn't so little anymore. Bianca weighed more than twenty pounds at her one-year checkup."

"Good thing you're used to dealing with heavyweights." Eve grinned, watching the tiny woman easily heft a large bag of flour out of the shopping cart.

"You're certainly doing your holiday baking early. It's only November 30th," Maria observed, piling sugar, red and green sprinkles and walnuts next to the flour.

"Well, it's hard to resist getting ready for the season when the whole town's had Christmas decorations up since Halloween." Eve pointed to the cheerful holiday trappings all around the store. "But this stuff is for the confirmation class at St. Junipero. They're in charge of the cookie concession at the bazaar this weekend and..."

"And you're donating the ingredients," Maria finished for her.

"Oh, it's only a little dough for a good cause," Eve deadpanned, joining Maria in the groan her bad pun required.

"But you're not even Catholic, are you?" Maria observed, waiting while the cash register took a few seconds to calculate the total.

"No, but I've known Father Moreno for years. He used to play chess with my dad at our house every week. And I owe him a lot."

Like gratitude for helping me survive all of last year's disasters, Eve thought. She fought back a sudden wave of sadness with a rush of words. "I mean, he's sent a lot of people my way, like your sister. When you own a house as old as mine... Well, the extra money I make playing at weddings and such really makes a difference in keeping it up."

"It's such a beautiful adobe." Maria nodded. "I love the wonderful garden in back. Every time I visit, I just want to sit there and watch the butterflies all day. I can understand not wanting to let your house deteriorate. But, *chica,* I hope you're taking time out for a little fun, too. Are you dating anybody special?"

Eve schooled her face not to show the stab of pain Maria's gentle probing provoked. She rubbed her bare ring finger again. The engagement diamond that had glittered there had been gone long enough that the band of white skin marring her tan had disappeared.

It had been almost a year. A year since her parents died; a year since walking into the upstairs studio the night after the funeral and...

Shaking her head hard enough to loosen a few long, honey-blond strands from their restraining clip, Eve finally answered her friend. "No, Maria, I haven't met anyone special."

Yet, even as she said the words, her eyes found the tall man who rounded a nearby aisle and then charged down it toward the far end.

Maria's gaze followed. "Wow! Now there's a pair of shoulders you don't often see outside of 'Monday Night Football'! I bet he's new in town, and no stranger to doing his own grocery shopping," she assessed after her quick glance at the loaded cart. Maria looked back at Eve, an expectant grin lighting her delicate features. "Are you going to wait here until he finishes?"

"Uh-uh, definitely not my type." Trying not to admit how tempted she really was, Eve just smiled innocently at her friend and whipped out her checkbook.

Out in the parking lot, she forced herself not to look back while she quickly put her groceries in the car and then set off for her home in nearby Pacific Grove.

THE NEXT MORNING Eve stood in the middle of her kitchen gulping down coffee. After rinsing out the cup in the sink, she glanced at the wall clock. Seven-thirty already. She could hardly believe it was time to head back to work again. *What a rat race,* she thought as she rushed into the living room to grab her purse from the end table near the vestibule door.

Her eyes automatically roamed the gracefully proportioned room with its wide-plank flooring and exposed white ceiling beams. As had been the case recently, tears threatened.

She would never give in to Janet's demands. This historic adobe had appreciated dramatically in the past several years. Which was why her sister wanted it sold, the proceeds divided.

But Eve had refused. What did money mean to her when everything she had left to love in the world could be found in this room and the rest of the house?

She turned slowly. The thick, whitewashed walls were hung with paintings and woven tapestries in keeping with the classic Monterey style.

The huge fireplace, with its rough-hewn oak mantel, dominated one end of the room. Balancing it on the opposite side, floor-to-ceiling wood shelving housed a large collection of books and tapes, along with her father's stereo equipment. And in a large alcove between the fireplace and the bookshelves, Eve's concert grand piano gleamed.

Her parents had always raised the Christmas tree next to the piano. Some of Eve's most cherished memories were of singing carols with her family, the wonderful scent of pine tickling her nose, and multicolored shadows from the glass ornaments reflecting on the keyboard.

This year she didn't have the emotional strength to even think of putting up a tree, let alone decorate it with the beloved echoes of Christmases past. Last December's events had palled the meaning of the season for her.

PULLING OUT of the driveway a few minutes later, Eve opened her window, testing the air. While it was a bit chilly this morning, she allowed the salt-tanged breeze free reign in the little gold car. Turning onto Ocean View Boulevard, she followed the curving seaside road into Monterey and the government research facility where she worked.

There were quicker ways to cross over from Pacific Grove into Monterey proper, but she always enjoyed this route. Somehow, seeing the eternal pounding of the sea, while she drove, fortified her for the long hours spent cooped up in a tiny office, hunched over her computer terminal.

The streets leading into downtown Monterey weren't crowded this morning. But in another few weeks, when the annual waves of holiday tourists crested, driving would be bumper to bumper.

Turning off Del Monte Avenue, just before the Naval Postgraduate School, Eve used her security pass to open the guard barrier into the parking lot of the low, windowless communications building.

After pulling into a space, she made her way through the main entrance door and handed her pass to the baby-faced marine corporal on duty. Eve waited with a patient smile as he carefully checked her picture and the identification statistics on the back, just as he had done every workday for the past few weeks.

"Blond hair... really long and thick... yup. Green eyes... tilted like a cat's... okay. Height... five-feet, nine-inches... I'll say! Weight..."

"Within the accepted range, Corporal Dalinski," Eve interrupted with a laugh, just as she always did in response to the mild flirting. Thank God, he had stopped comparing her real face to the one in the photo. She hated how the picture exaggerated her high cheekbones and square chin, making her features look even stronger than they were in reality.

A few minutes later she pushed into her tiny office and plopped her briefcase down next to the computer terminal on her desk. Last night she had finished plotting the latest data that correlated the ascending and descending nodes of various earth-synchronous satellites. Now, to see if the data matched the experimental LinkUp model being tested, all she had to do was enter the results into the specialized software that would transform her work into easily understood graphs.

Eve was deep into the process when a knock on her door announced the entrance of two people. She looked up distractedly, and did a classic double take. Julie Rosen, the unit's bubbly, redheaded personnel officer stood there, right next to a huge, dark-haired man.

Rows of gibberish suddenly ran across Eve's screen when her fingers froze on the keyboard. The broad body that instantly dominated the room—the black hair, the dark, smiling eyes—all belonged to last night's stranger.

"Eve, I'd like you to meet Sam Davidson," Julie said. Eve watched bemused while her friend, standing slightly behind the man, rolled her eyes and made pitter-patter motions over her heart with her hand. "Sam's taking over from Terry as our new head of computer security. And I can't tell you how happy we are to have someone with his credentials on board."

The breathy, almost coquettish quality of the happily married woman's voice finally penetrated Eve's paralysis. She managed to rise and extend her hand while Julie completed the introductions.

"And, Sam, this is Eve Gray, one of our resident statisticians."

"Hello, Eve, happy to meet you . . . formally." The deep baritone made a caress of the greeting.

Long, strong fingers enclosed her hand for a quick, warm shake. The gorgeous smile—made slightly crooked by a small scar on his long upper lip—conveyed a remembrance of their brief musical encounter last evening in the Safeway parking lot.

But instead of embarrassing her by referring to it, Sam just said, "I wanted to say hello to everyone before I start cracking the whip on computer security."

His wonderful grin flashed, taking the sting out of the implied threat. Looking way up into eyes she just noticed were the darkest blue imaginable, Eve suddenly acknowledged the reality of fate, or karma, or destiny.

Even though she had chickened out last night at the supermarket, it seemed that some force was working to give her another chance to get to know this incredibly attractive man.

Eve knew she must have made some sort of intelligent reply and responded to Sam's questions satisfactorily, because neither he nor Julie looked at her strangely, or seemed to notice the wild, soaring flight her emotions were taking.

But a few minutes later her heart's skylarking journey ended in an abrupt crash when Sam stopped in the doorway to wave goodbye. The overhead fluorescent light picked up a glint of gold on his left hand.

It was only then Eve realized that Sam Davidson wore a wide, beautifully crafted wedding band.

Chapter One

"Eve, sorry I'm...so late. Joe and I just got back...from seeing our new granddaughter...in San Francisco," Hertha Jenkins said between huffs. She sank down on a cafeteria chair to catch her breath.

"You shouldn't have rushed like that, dear," Eve said, handing her friend some paper napkins from the nearby table dispenser.

"Well, I wanted to get this to you in time." She gave Eve a long paper cylinder, then wiped the moisture dotting her round, ebony-skinned face. "It's what I volunteered to do for tonight's party decorations. Happy New Year written in Tibetan. I had a hard time finding the information until my husband had the brilliant idea of going to that lamasery up north. The people there were very helpful."

"Oh, Hertha, it's wonderful." Excess glitter rained down on Eve's denim shirt and jeans when she unrolled the tube of paper. She held up the sign to examine the intricate pictographs more closely. "Just beautiful. Trust you to do things right. I'm glad you didn't have to go all the way to Tibet for the correct translation."

"So am I. My first choice—Portuguese—would have been a whole lot easier to do," the facility's lead programmer said with a smile, and then pointed to her banner. "Do you want me to put this up with the rest of the signs?"

"Oh, Tom's doing that. You take it easy. I'll just go over and have him hang it in a place of honor," Eve said, taking a few steps before she looked back over her shoulder. "By the way, congratulations on the birth of your new grandchild. That's number..."

"Three. They named her Melody Anne. Nine pounds, seven ounces. My daughter swears this is the last one." A big grin spread across Hertha's plump face. "But then, she always says the same thing until the stitches heal."

Eve was still chuckling when she reached Tom Lewis at the other end of the cafeteria. The young electronics engineer had just gotten down from an eight-foot ladder.

"Not another one, Eve," he groaned, looking at what she had in her hands.

"This is the last of them, I promise. Come on, bring the ladder. There's a great space for this sign to the right of the entry where everyone will see it. I'll spot for you. I get so nervous when you go up that thing without someone bracing it."

"Oh, I do this all the time in the communications center. You know how often something goes wrong with the wiring up above the false ceiling," he said, easily scrambling up the rungs once again. "Is the sign straight, Eve?"

"Hold on, Tom, let me get back a bit. Now, don't you move," she warned, taking a few steps away. "Up a little on the left. Okay, perfect. Tape it and get down from there.''

Rushing back to steady the ladder while Tom descended, Eve blew a wayward strand of blond hair out of her eyes and checked on the activities of the other people milling around the cafeteria.

Administration had declared an official ''Dress Down Day,'' which meant everyone wore casual clothing. Hard to believe that in just a few hours they had transformed the windowless, rather Spartan room into the Café: It's A Small World. Her planning committee had borrowed from the Disney theme to celebrate tonight's test of Project LinkUp.

Each table in the cafeteria featured a flag and some sort of decoration representing a particular country. The banners Tom had just finished putting up glittered with the words Happy New Year in two dozen languages.

''Looking good,'' Eve said to herself, and then raised her voice. ''Okay, everybody, thank you all for a great job. Go home and get some rest. I'll meet the food committee here at nine p.m. to set up the buffet.''

Watching her volunteers pack up to leave, Eve felt herself wilting at the thought of coming back for the late-night celebration. With one thing and another, December had been a very tough month for her. Thank God, New Year's Eve was falling on a Friday; she had a three-day weekend coming up.

''Eve, Eve, get over here, quick!''

''Now what?'' she muttered. Turning toward the excited hail, Eve saw that Hertha had joined Julie Rosen and Tawny Bronsen at a table across the room.

The three women called themselves The Monterey Yenta Association. They lived for gossip. Yet, for all their love of rumor and scandal, there wasn't a malicious bone in any of them, and Eve counted the trio among her best friends.

She just didn't have their avid interest in snooping, so Eve resisted falling prey to their group obsession. She jokingly used her status as a Pacific Grove resident to disqualify herself from official membership in the little club.

"Guess what we just found out," Julie stage-whispered after Eve plopped down on a chair. "She's definitely coming to the New Year's Eve party tonight."

"Who's coming?" Eve dutifully asked the personnel officer, although she had a sinking feeling she knew just what Julie was so thrilled about.

"Amber Davidson, Sam's wife," Tawny broke in. "Now we'll finally find out what she's got that makes him totally oblivious to other women."

Given Tawny's statuesque body and perfect features, Eve could understand why the raven-haired cryptographer had never before experienced such a lack of male response.

The indignant look on Tawny's beautiful face made Eve laugh out loud. It felt good, because she had not had a whole lot to laugh about in the four weeks since Sam's arrival.

"Eve, you don't have to be on duty tonight when they juice up the whatsits, do you?" Hertha asked. The energetic grandmother liked to project a scatter-brained image. But everyone using her computer programs knew a first-class mind resided under her curly graying hair.

"No, I won't have to help analyze the LinkUp data they download until we get back to work on Tuesday," Eve answered. "But I'm not so sure I'm going to make the party, anyway. I'm really pooped. All these late nights, and then working on the committee . . ."

"Eve, you've got to come!" Julie cut into her feeble excuses. "After all you did to organize the event, don't you want to take a bow? Besides, there'll be lots of gorgeous single guys here tonight. Why don't you give them a thrill by wearing something tight and cut down to your *pippik?* That's Yiddish for belly button, in case you didn't know."

Eve's head snapped up at the phrase "single guys." Hertha and Tawny were nodding their agreement with Julie. Did that mean they all knew how she felt about Sam? Shoot, she had tried so hard to be careful!

"Forget about tight dresses," Hertha chided, scattering Eve's troubled thoughts. "I still say we should have made this a costume party. That way I could have come as an African queen and worn a comfortable, but oh, so flattering, robe."

"I, of course, would get out my diamond tiara and be the Jewish American Princess," Julie giggled, running with the theme. "Tawny could come as a Valkyrie . . . While Eve—"

"Would don pointy alien ears, paint my skin green, and go as *Ms. Spock,* the Vulcan," Eve suggested with a grin—well-aware of the nickname people at the facility had pinned on her.

Julie's face turned that shade of pink only a true redhead can achieve, but she then patted Eve's hand. "Nobody means anything bad by that silly name. It's just the way you sometimes talk, dear. You know—so precise, so logical"

Yeah, sure, Eve thought wryly. So logical that she had gone and fallen for a married man!

But seeing the pain in Julie's eyes, she hastened to reassure her friend. "Oh, that moniker doesn't bother me."

And it really didn't. Because, as Julie had just said, there was no malice in the teasing title. Unlike the label her sister Janet had pasted on Eve's damaged heart one miserable morning last December.

"I know how analytical I can sound." She forced herself to continue. "But it's just how my mind works...very linear. My dad used to say that I was the best, and worst, chess player he'd ever seen. I could visualize a dozen moves ahead, but couldn't plan alternate strategies to save my soul." Eve smiled at the memory of how exasperated her father would get during their matches.

"That's because you're so up-front, so straightforward," Hertha chimed in. "Why, there isn't a devious bone in your body, girl! With you, what you see is what you get."

But you're wrong, Hertha, Eve wanted to shout in denial. She did know how to be devious, at least where Sam Davidson was concerned. Because it was now obvious to Eve that she *had* kept her feelings about Sam a secret these past few weeks, even from these three perceptive women.

Julie's comment about dressing to attract a *single* man had only meant that she thought it was time for Eve to get on with her life and forget about the disastrous end of her engagement to Steven Lange last year.

"Well, thank you, ladies, for your endorsement," Eve found herself saying with a rush of affection for them. "And on second thought, I'd kick myself if I didn't come tonight and get a look at the mysterious Amber Davidson."

To tell the truth, for almost a month she had listened in with covert interest while this feminine contingent discussed the Davidsons during lunch.

At first the topic had been Sam's dreamboat status. The other women had spent days playfully making a detailed list of his obvious attractions. Then they had engaged in wild speculation about hidden attributes.

But what had really piqued their interest was trying to find out something more about his wife, beyond her name.

"Well, heaven knows I did everything I could think of to get Sam to open up about Amber," Julie said, hitching a ride on Eve's train of thought. "He must have been a clam in his last incarnation. If it weren't unethical, I'd have accessed the computer files to dig up something about the woman."

"Instead you just *nudged* the poor guy to death for the information," Hertha teased.

"Guilty, I admit it, for all the good it did me. He didn't tell me a thing that wasn't on his résumé. And all it says is, he graduated with a major in computer engineering from the University of Michigan, and he has a master's degree from U.C., San Diego. Then, after serving as a weapons officer on the *Kitty Hawke,* he mustered out a year ago with the rank of lieutenant commander. And from his I-9 form, I found out he's thirty-two. That's it . . . sum total knowledge."

Eve hadn't even known that much about Sam. Thirty-two? Nine years older than herself. His snub nose and Irish face made him look much younger.

"But, Eve—" Julie turned toward her "—I've seen him talking to you several times here in the cafeteria. Are you sure he never mentioned his wife during those coffee breaks?"

Eve immediately got busy brushing the wayward glitter from Hertha's banner off her jeans, hoping no one saw the blush burning her cheeks.

When she felt the heat recede, she looked up and tried to hide her true feelings in her most precise imitation of a Star Trek Vulcan. "Oh, he's never talked about anything personal to me. Beyond the fact, like you said, that he's originally from Michigan, and they moved here from San Diego. The topic is usually computer security, or books. He's a science fiction nut, like me."

But it was true he *did* seem to go out of his way to talk with her. And, at first, Eve thought Sam might be initiating the one-on-one discussions with seduction in mind.

The suspicion had put her on the horns of a moral dilemma of monumental proportions.

On the one hand, she hated the idea of infidelity. A commitment was a commitment, especially one of the heart . . . and of the body. Her experience with Janet and Steven had only reinforced the deeply held conviction.

Yet on the other hand, every time she had talked with Sam in those first few days, each time she even looked at him, Eve felt such a rush of emotion—such a sense of rightness in being with him—she constantly had to remind herself that he was out of bounds.

Thankfully, she never revealed her runaway attraction to him, because it took her only a week to decide her fears about Sam's motives were groundless. He talked to her for one reason alone—because he *liked* her. As a friend.

Oh, she had been glad. She had been relieved. Only nobody bothered to tell her subconscious how she felt.

As a result, in the past few weeks her dreams had taken on an erotic intensity she had never before experienced. And there was nothing hazy about her nighttime fantasies. They starred Sam Davidson, ready and rampant . . . Eve Gray, willing and pliant.

The dreams made her even more aware of Sam. Her ears recognized the timbre of his deep voice in any babble of conversation. Her very skin seemed to know when he came into the crowded cafeteria.

In fact, a couple of days ago she had been walking down the white-tiled corridors behind the testing lab when the hair on the back of her neck stood up. Looking around, she saw Sam a few paces back, reading some sort of report as he strode down the hallway.

Even as she snapped her head back around to the front, Eve tripped on her own feet. She would have fallen headfirst into the wall, if it hadn't been for his strong hands, which pulled her back from disaster.

Afterward, gazing up into Sam's dark blue eyes, Eve almost lost it. All she'd wanted to do was put her arms around his neck and never let go. Instead, hoping her desire hadn't been reflected in her eyes, she'd mumbled her thanks and left his vicinity as fast as she could.

The experience had made her certain that, inevitably, she was going to screw up. One day, sooner or later, she would say something, or do something, that would let her friends—or Sam—know just how obsessed she was with him.

Which was why, as much as she dreaded it, she *was* going to introduce herself to Amber Davidson tonight. She prayed that after seeing the two of them together—after Amber became a real person to Eve—she would have taken the first step in recovery from her overwhelming desire for the woman's husband.

"Well, ladies, I'm going home to soak in a bubble bath and then get me some beauty sleep," Tawny informed the group, rising from her chair. "Got to look good enough to break a few hearts tonight."

"Wish a little sleep could do it for me," Hertha groaned, patting her double chin and pushing herself to her feet.

"Oh, I've seen the way your Joe looks at you, Hertha," Julie countered. "And I'd say Amber Davidson isn't the only gal around here with a one-woman man."

Hertha and Amber should coauthor a book on how to identify members of that rare male species...they'd make a fortune, Eve thought wryly as she walked with her friends to the parking lot.

IT WAS ALMOST SIX when Eve let herself into her house, but she hadn't been home this early in weeks. Thinking Tawny's plan for a nice hot bath and a nap sounded wonderful, she tossed her purse and the mail on the end table next to the couch.

Some music would also be nice, she thought, walking across the room toward the tape deck.

Passing the alcove that housed her piano, Eve found herself regretting her decision not to have a Christmas tree this year.

She had thought remembrances of happier holiday seasons would make her depressed. Well, she hadn't put up any decorations, and she still felt down. The only hints of the season were the many cards from friends and co-workers vying for room on the fireplace mantel among family photographs.

Of course, there wasn't a greeting from Janet and Steven. Eve hadn't sent a card to them, either. And even if she had wanted to, she wasn't sure where they were living. Had they moved into a bigger apartment in Berkeley? Steven's place near the University of California campus had been so tiny.

Eve's eyes felt the sudden acid burn of all the tears she had been unable to shed this year. Whirling away from the tape deck without turning it on, she went into the bedroom and stripped off her clothing.

She had moved into the master suite just a few weeks ago. Upon inheriting the house after the plane crash last year, she hadn't been able to even think of changing a thing.

Finally realizing that her parents would not have wanted her to make a shrine of this place—it was a house designed for living, not grieving—she'd started with plans to redecorate the master bedroom.

Keeping the solid antique furniture, she had sewn new draperies and found a bright, intricately quilted bedspread for the enormous bed.

Yawning widely, she walked into the en suite bathroom that had been added during her grandparents' day and decided a shower might be better than a bath. Tired as she was, she'd have absolutely no problem falling asleep.

After showering and drying her hair, she picked up the bedside clock. Eve acknowledged her tendency to turn off the buzzer and go right back to sleep by setting the double alarm option to ring at eight and five after eight.

Really should put the clock out of arm's reach, she thought for the umpteenth time, and then sleepily sank down onto the bed.

But Eve didn't have any trouble getting up at the first alarm. She hadn't slept deeply, at all. Crazy dreams of chasing Sam down twisting, mirrored corridors had haunted her sleep. After splashing her face with cold water in an attempt to wash away the last remnants of the nightmares, she retrieved her party outfit from the large wardrobe opposite the bed.

Her forest green cocktail dress didn't have the low cleavage Julie had suggested, but Eve felt satisfied it fit well and suited her full-figured body. The wide belt that nipped in her small waist emphasized her generous breasts and hips; the effect was feminine, rather than blatantly sexy.

Three-inch heels, dyed to match the dress, finished the outfit and brought Eve's height to six feet. For the most part, she didn't try to hide her size, and these narrow green pumps made her legs look long and elegant.

"Amazon! You're a big, fat Amazon!"

Janet's harsh voice suddenly rang loud in Eve's memory. She didn't flash back to that day last year very often, but it shook her every time it happened.

With her hands still trembling, Eve took a long time finishing her makeup, light though it was. Then she tried to decide what to do with her hair. The thick, sun-streaked blond mass fell well below her waist.

First, she plaited it into a long rope and coiled it on top of her head.

But with Janet's hateful words still fresh in her mind, the thought of towering over most everyone tonight didn't appeal to her very much.

After trying a chignon and then a French braid, Eve finally admitted to stalling, postponing the moment when she had to face the Davidsons. Sighing, she just stuck a few crystal-decorated hairpins into the French braid to finish her handiwork. Gathering up her green satin purse and a wool shawl, Eve hurried to the kitchen refrigerator to retrieve the multilayered taco salad that was her contribution to the potluck buffet.

ARRIVING a half hour late to the party, Eve put her shawl and purse in her office, and then rushed into the cafeteria with her taco salad bowl in hand. But it seemed the volunteers had set up without her, and things were going smoothly.

Some people were already lined up for the food, while at the near end of the room, a large group had gathered in front of Julie's husband, Bob Rosen. Although his training as a pediatrician seemed far afield, the Paul Newman look-alike had volunteered to act as DJ for the evening. At the moment, he was "scratching" a record like a professional. However, his rap had a strange reggae twist to it.

"Now everybody peep game and let me tell you a little story about Tom, Mon." Bob pointed to Tom Lewis, who stood in the crowd. "Engineer Tom is the guy who makes the dynamos hum, Mon. They go hum, Mon. But if his fingers miss and the wires go hiss... it gets dark, Mon. Really dark, Mon. From Monterey to New Jer-say, it gets dark, Mon. Boy, it's dark, Mon!"

About to join the rest of the crowd in clapping for Bob's improvisational rap, Eve realized she still had a taco salad in her hands that needed delivering to the buffet. The sudden growling of her stomach also reminded her that lunch had been a long, long time ago.

Heading for the food-laden tables, she apologized to the volunteers for being late, and then located a space for the bowl. Surveying the bounty, Eve took a plate and piled it high with a variety of the ethnic foods that were part of tonight's theme. Looking around the room, she found the table where Julie and Tawny had taken up residence.

"Hello, ladies. You both look terrific," Eve greeted her friends and slid into an empty chair. Julie wore a sophisticated, royal blue coatdress that complemented her dark red hair and petite frame, while Tawny answered every man's dream in a tightly fitted black number that revealed a good deal of creamy skin.

"Not too bad yourself," Tawny decided with a quick scan of Eve's green outfit.

"Say, Julie," Eve said around a mouthful of food, "Bob's doing a terrific job over there. Your gorgeous husband could give up his practice and make a fortune as an entertainer. He really is something."

"*Oy vey,* don't encourage him! Just what the world needs, another Jewish reggae rapper!"

Trying not to choke on her laughter—or food, Eve finally managed to swallow. "Oh, you are a dangerous woman, Julie. And speaking of hazardous females, where's Hertha . . . and Joe?"

"She called me at home and said they'd be about an hour late," Tawny piped up. "Joe's restaurant is awfully busy tonight, but his manager is going to take over at ten. Anyway, I've saved them a couple of seats."

She pointed to the pair among the remaining vacant chairs that had been tipped toward the table.

"Good," Eve nodded. "And so are these potato pancakes. Julie, are these yours?"

"Yes, and by the way, they're called potato *latkes*, you incorrigible WASP. Serving them on New Year's Eve is a tradition on the Romanian side of Bob's family. He made me take lessons from his *bubbe* before he'd marry me. I had to go to his grandmother's house every Friday for weeks, until I could finally make them just right."

"Ah, what we won't do for love," Tawny taunted with a mischievous smile.

What wouldn't I do for love? Sam's love? Eve thought before she could censor herself. Her initial enthusiasm for the various ethnic treats on her plate abruptly died. She found that she was picking at the food, and not because she lacked an adventurous palate.

She hoped nobody noticed how nervous she felt. Probably not. Julie sat watching her husband's antics with an indulgent expression on her freckled face. Tawny had just come back from dancing with the facility doctor, Dennis Hartcourt, and still chatted with the man.

The two had dated at one time, but Tawny was dedicated to playing the field until, as she put it, she met the man who would "melt her socks off."

"How about a whirl around the floor, Eve?" Dennis asked when Tawny went off to dance with a marine captain.

"Sure, thank you." She got up and followed him to the area set aside for dancing. "So, how's the doctoring business going, Dennis?"

"Same old, same old. Not much challenge around here. This is a very healthy bunch of people, for the most part. But last week I did have an interesting case of..."

As Dennis went on and on about a carpal tunnel syndrome victim he was treating, Eve's mind shifted into automatic.

The same thing happened every time she dated Dennis. The sandy-haired doctor had asked her out a few times, on the rebound from capricious Tawny, she suspected. Eve had accepted, but only after making it very clear to him she just wanted to be friends. He had been all too happy to agree.

And it soon became obvious to both of them that they didn't really have anything in common. Absolutely no sparks had been generated between them during their few evenings together.

When she got back to the table, Eve joined in on a lively conversation with her companions. But she knew the instant Sam Davidson entered the room; a fierce wave of longing suddenly washed over her.

She swiveled in her seat and saw him standing in the entrance. In one hand he held a large paper bag. His other arm was draped around the shoulders of a tall, very thin redheaded woman clad in a brightly colored, floor-length sarong. Although music still played loudly, it seemed the room fell silent and every eye turned toward the couple in the doorway.

As if fate were somehow punishing Eve for coveting a married man, his wife scanned the cafeteria and then pointed directly at her.

Chapter Two

Watching the Davidsons slowly cross the floor toward her, Eve's eyes widened in surprise. Amber Davidson limped, badly.

"Hello, everybody. Sorry we're late. The dessert refused to cooperate," Sam announced, holding up the paper bag. "Amber, this is Julie and Tawny and Eve. The lucky gentleman with them is Dr. Dennis Hartcourt. Everyone, I'd like you to meet my wife, Amber."

The woman smiled and touched her hair with a nervous gesture. Eve noted whereas Julie's red hair glowed with mahogany highlights, Amber's shade blared bright orange. Cut short, it curled into tight corkscrews that—together with her big blue eyes and deep-set dimples—reminded Eve of Little Orphan Annie. She immediately chastised herself for the catty thought.

"G'day all. Took one look at the Aussie Blue flag here with the cute koala bear hanging on it and I knew this had to be our table," Amber announced in a broad Australian accent. "May we join you?"

Julie Rosen, like the good personnel officer she was, overcame her astonishment first. "Yes, of course!

There's plenty of room," she said, jumping up and pulling out a chair. "Come on, Amber, you sit down right between Eve and me. Sam, why don't you... Oh, look, there's Hertha and Joe. Over here, Hertha, we've saved you places."

In the confusion of arranging seating, Eve had time to compose herself. Talk about a case of galloping paranoia! Of course, Amber hadn't directed Sam to this table because she wanted to chew out Eve for fancying her husband.

Amber had merely spotted the deep blue Australian flag—with its bright red Union Jack and five white stars set in the pattern of the Southern Cross. Naturally, she would choose to sit at the table representing her native country.

But then Eve had another disturbing thought. Just why had her friends picked *this* particular spot to sit? All at once, she had the feeling fate had been busy shuffling life's cards again, dealing her another rotten hand.

"Amber, this is Hertha and Joe Jenkins," Sam introduced the other latecomers. "I think I've mentioned Hertha . . ."

"Right'o, you're the programming whiz," Amber said with a wide smile, highlighting her charming dimples. "Sam says he'd be up to the dunny without a newspaper if you hadn't understood just what kind of computer security programs he wanted. And, Joe, I can't remember, do you work here, too?"

"No, I own a restaurant down in Cannery Row. The Hungry Seagull," Hertha's tall, cadaverous husband said.

It was hard for Eve not to think of Jack Sprat and his wife when she saw the couple together. Fattening food was the delight and bane of Hertha's existence. Her relationship with Joe's restaurant was an ambivalent one, to say the least.

"Well, Sam and I will have to go there some night soon. And speaking of food..." Amber turned to her husband, "Sam, lovey, why don't you take the pavlova over to the buffet before it's ruined. Don't forget to ladle the whipped cream and fruit on top."

"Sure, honey. And I'll bring back something for us to eat."

"That'd be beaut, sweetheart. But light'o on the tucker for me."

Amber's reply bordered on gibberish to Eve, but Sam seemed to understand. With one of his gorgeous smiles, he strode off toward the buffet. Eve had to force her eyes back to his wife.

"When I heard we were supposed to bring along a plate," Amber was saying to the rest of the table, "I just had to make a pavlova. Wouldn't seem like New Year's Eve without one. National puddin' of Australia, at least in the western part where I come from. Spent a fortune for the kiwis, and I think the grocer diddled me."

Into the silence that remark engendered, Hertha piped up, "Joe, why don't you go get us some tucker, too? But don't be afraid to pile mine high and deep. Especially that beaut pavlova."

"Good on yer! How do you know Strine?" Amber asked Hertha, blue eyes widening.

"Oh, I'm addicted to romance novels. Lots of them take place in Australia, so I've picked up some of your unique vocabulary. For example, I know that 'diddled' means cheated, and 'dunny' is an outhouse," Hertha explained, grinning at the other Americans.

"And I've read about pavlovas in dozens of my books. But I never could figure out exactly how they were made."

"Well, they're mostly meringue, whipped cream and fruit." Amber quickly went through the recipe for Hertha. "A lot of people top it with strawberries, but I'm deathly allergic to them, so I use kiwi fruit instead."

Her fingers patted her bright hair again in that nervous gesture. Eve noticed for the first time that Amber's long, thin fingers and delicate wrists were bedecked with the most unusual jewelry she had ever seen. Half shellwork, half gold, it seemed as if someone had taken the bounty of the sea and earth and combined it into unique works of art. Sam's wedding ring was of the same sort of design, and identical to the one that Amber wore on her left hand.

Remembering her vow to make Amber into a real person in her mind, Eve forced herself to engage the woman in conversation. But within a few minutes she was so captivated by her warm personality, Eve only vaguely noticed when Tawny and Dennis went off to dance. And she reacted almost normally when Sam returned with a plate of food for his wife, and then went to sit across the table with the Jenkinses.

As the night progressed, Eve found that Amber's accent became less broad, and she didn't pat her hair anymore. *Why, she was as nervous of meeting us as I was of meeting her!* Eve belatedly figured out. Amber's use of so many "Australianisms" must have been a bravura performance in which she could safely hide her insecurities. The thought sent a wave of warm empathy stealing into Eve's heart.

"I couldn't help noticing your jewelry, Amber," she said at the next opportunity. "I've never seen anything so beautiful. Did you find it in Australia?"

"Oh, I made this stuff. I've fiddled around with doing this sort of thing for years."

"Don't let her fool you, Eve," Sam broke in, almost as if he had been keeping close tabs on their conversation. "Amber's an award-winning jewelry designer. And it's only one of the crafts she's known for in Australia and the Orient. Among other things, my talented wife also creates a line of fabrics, like the one she used for her dress."

He nodded to her evening sarong. Its whimsically colored flowers should have clashed with Amber's hair, but somehow they complemented it instead.

"Oh, stop, dear. You're making me seem like a tall poppy," Amber protested with a wave of her bangled hands.

"Tall poppy?" Eve asked.

"That's something very Australian. We're so democratic over there, nobody wants to seem better than anyone else. So overachievers get cut down to size . . . like tall poppies, if you see what I mean."

"Yes, I understand what you're saying." Eve nodded her head. "But doesn't that go against human nature? Oh, excuse me, Amber. I didn't mean . . ."

"Don't worry, ducks. You're right. It's hard being different. I'd been cut down all my life, and I guess I was sick of it. Sure left the place in a hurry when my Sam arrived on the scene."

"How *did* you and Sam meet?" Julie asked. Her big brown eyes were bright with the hope she finally might get the information she'd craved for weeks.

"Oh, it's a wonderful story. But probably long and boring to anyone except Sam and me. So those who want to should get out while they can."

"Not on your life!" Julie all but shouted, and then turned bright red.

Eve joined in the laughter circling the table, but like everyone else, she waited expectantly for Amber's tale.

"Well, don't say you weren't warned. I guess you should know I was born on a sheep station outback in the never-never. But my ma got sick of my pot and all the lanolin, and divorced him. When she remarried, I spent half the year with her in the Abrolhos Islands, north of Perth, setting lobster traps on my stepdad's boat. It was great fun, living right on the ocean for weeks at a time, and only having to go to school a couple of hours a day by way of the radio service.

"Anyway, I'd find all these shells and seaweed, and other things along with the lobsters we pulled up. I'd stick them together in ways I liked, and soon found out other people liked them, too…and would pay for the stuff. Had quite a business going by the time I was sixteen. But then my pot decided I was turning into a fair dinkum laze-about and demanded I get some formal schooling. I wasn't too happy about it, but wouldn't you know it, my ma agrees with the old man for the first time in history. So off I go to Perth and then the Uni."

"And that's where you met Sam?" Hertha broke in. "At the university…uh, Uni?"

"I'm getting to that, told you it was a long story," Amber said, dimples deepening. "But since it's getting late, I'll condense a bit. The girls at my boarding house decided to Dial-a-Sailor."

"Dial-a..." Julie began, then waved her hand in the air. "Sorry, Amber. Please do go on."

"Yes, well, you see, there's lots of American navy guys stationed at Freo...Freemantle, which is the port for Perth. And a mutual admiration society has sort of grown up. People love to invite the sailors for a home-cooked meal. So the city set up an agency...Dial-a-Sailor. You can call them and ask for one or more navy guests. And I can tell you, we girls called often. When compared to your garden variety Australian chauvinist, Americans are beauts. Your guys don't have a chance. And you didn't, either, did you, Boomer?"

"Nary a one," Sam agreed, a flush of red highlighting his cheeks at the obviously intimate nickname. The love radiating between the couple seemed to warm the whole table.

Eve fought to keep her own cheeks from burning. How could she ever have let herself fantasize about this man? The only thing she wanted to do now was go home to bed and hide her head under the covers for a week . . . a month. Maybe the rest of her life!

But before she could move, Sam got up and came around the table. Eve hoped no one noticed her cringe when his hand accidentally brushed against her bare arm as he leaned over to talk with his wife.

"Honey, it's almost eleven," he told Amber. "I've got to make one last check on computer security before the big test at midnight. I might be a while. Do you want to go home, or stay here?"

"Oh, I'm having too good a time to go back to that dinky apartment." Amber then slowly, painfully, got up and put her long, thin arms around her husband's neck. "Sam, I'll let you go, but first we're going to dance. We haven't danced since our wedding, three years ago!''

"Amber, it's too soon. It's only three months since your last operation."

"Nonsense, I've been swimming for weeks now. Swim like a fish," she confided to Eve. "May dance like one, too. But let's give it a try."

Eve watched, unable to tear her eyes away when Sam nodded and then carefully guided his wife to the dance floor.

Bob Rosen had just put on something slow and dreamy. Sam took Amber into his arms, holding her as if she were a precious gem.

For the first time Eve wondered about Amber's disability. When the Davidsons had walked in, Eve had been too nervous to do anything but note the limp. And then, for the past hour, Amber's delightful personality had made Eve forget all about her condition.

But now she wondered if the latest operation Sam mentioned was to treat some congenital problem, or if the Australian woman had been in an accident that required ongoing, reconstructive surgery.

Whatever the cause, Eve felt tears come to her eyes. Amber's analogy about dancing like a fish made her think of the Little Mermaid, whose every step was taken in pain. Pain and love. And while watching them together out on the dance floor, Eve got her wish.

She knew she now had the strength to seal away her feelings for Sam behind an impregnable barrier. She could be his friend . . . and wish for nothing more.

From across the room, almost as if he had heard her silent vow, Sam's dark eyes locked with Eve's for a strange, intense instant.

It couldn't have been longer than that, because when Eve immediately felt a violent shudder run through her body, she squeezed her lids shut. *Oh, Lord, don't let me break down now,* she prayed fervently.

But in the next second, the whole table began to shake. Eve's eyes flew open when glasses and plates crashed to the floor. She realized this was not the beginning of an emotional crack-up, but an earthquake.

All around her, people were shouting. Out of the corner of her eye, Eve watched Sam sweep Amber into his arms and stride with her toward the nearest exit.

Then, as quickly as it had started, the tremor ended.

"Wow...that was either right under us, or a big one hit a couple hundred miles away," Joe said, helping Hertha out of her chair.

"You don't think it could be in San Francisco, do you?" Hertha asked, her eyes wide with fright. "Joe, let's get to a phone and call Sarah."

"Hertha, don't get your blood pressure up. We don't even know where the epicenter was."

"Why don't we all go to the communications room, and find out where the quake did hit?" Eve suggested.

To her surprise, when Hertha mentioned her daughter in San Francisco, the first thing that came to Eve's mind had been her concern for her own sister's well-being. Whatever Janet had done, Eve guessed she couldn't wish her any harm.

"Well, what are we waiting for?" Hertha demanded, making for the cafeteria's exit at a speed Eve didn't think the older woman was capable of. Joe ran quickly after her.

Seeing she was the only one left at the table, Eve looked around at the milling crowd of confused people. She couldn't spot Tawny or Dennis, but she saw that Julie had rushed over to her husband. She was helping Bob sift through the pile of records that had fallen on the floor, trying to salvage what they could.

Following the Jenkinses to the communications room, Eve had to squeeze into it when she got there. Dozens of other people had obviously had the same idea.

Security protocol seemed to have been suspended. No one asked to see her ID badge, which was good, because she had left it stowed in her purse, in her office desk drawer.

Looking at the banks of monitors running up one wall, Eve saw that almost all of them showed only a snow pattern. Obviously the links had been cut to the sources of those signals. *Not a good sign,* she thought.

"Where did it hit, and what was the magnitude?" someone asked.

"Was it local?" another voice called out.

"...indicate a strong earthquake hit the San Francisco area at five minutes after eleven, Pacific standard time. This is CNN," an announcer's voice boomed, when one of the monitors came back on line.

"Stay tuned for more information as it's received. To repeat, all we know is that a strong earthquake has shaken the San—"

"Tom, can we use the phones here?" Hertha asked the young engineer hurrying by.

"Phones are either out or overloaded, Mrs. Jenkins. Excuse me, I've got to go up and check out the wiring for damage. Don't know if we can still run the experiment."

Tom hastened toward a scaffolding set against one wall and quickly climbed to the twelve-foot-high false ceiling. He pushed back a section of plastic paneling and crawled inside.

"But my daughter's in San Francisco... with her new baby," Hertha called after him, even as he disappeared. Looking dazed, she buried her face in her husband's jacket. "Oh, Joe, what should we do?"

"Now, now, sugar. Don't worry, Sarah and the kids are just fine. Do you want to go home and try to call from there?"

"All personnel. Attention, all facility personnel." A loudspeaker crackled to life overhead. "Preliminary reports just in indicate a 7.1 earthquake, lasting approximately thirty seconds, has occurred on the Hayward Fault. The cities of Berkeley and Oakland are the most affected. Reports of heavy road and building damage are coming in... casualty numbers has not been released ..."

Berkeley! That's where Janet and Steven probably were. Eve felt a chill run down her spine. What if they still lived in that old, brick apartment? Those were the kinds of buildings most likely to be damaged in a quake.

"We now have a live feed from our reporter in the East Bay area of San Francisco, where an earthquake, tentatively put at 7.1 on the Richter scale, occurred on the Hayward Fault about fifteen minutes ago," the CNN monitor erupted again.

A technician went to turn the volume down, but protests from the onlookers stayed his hand.

"John Jacobs has found a helicopter to fly him over the Berkeley area, east of San Francisco. What you will see is live. Our experts say this quake will be much more destructive to the Bay area than the 1989 Loma Prieta 7.1 temblor, because the epicenter is so much closer. We have no voice-over, so we'll try to interpret what is shown."

There was a brief flicker and then a slightly out-of-focus picture bobbed on the screen.

"That's a section of freeway fallen over on its side," the news anchor intoned. "And now we're seeing a block of buildings. Smoke or dust is rising from the collapsed structures. You can see people wandering down this street. There's . . . Oh, no . . . a tilting building just gave way and fell . . ."

"Oh, Joe, Eve. This is just awful," Hertha moaned.

"Take it easy, dear," Eve soothed, patting her friend's shoulder. "I'm sure your daughter is all right. She's across the Bay, and things are probably better over there."

But even as she said the comforting words, Eve's eyes strained to recognize some sort of landmark on the monitor. Lord, she had spent four years studying at the University of California in Berkeley. Why couldn't she figure out exactly where this damage was in the city?

"They kept saying this would happen." Joe shook his head. "But why didn't they know the fault was going to give tonight? I'm sure I read a few years ago the geologists were going to start issuing advanced warnings."

"I don't know," Eve answered distractedly, her eyes still focused on the screen. "Didn't they close down the prediction experiment over in Parkfield last year for lack of funds?"

"Yeah, they did. Damn fools." Joe swore. "Come on, Hertha, let's get home and try to call Sarah. Eve, want us to take you home, too?"

"Oh, no, Joe, thanks. I'll be all right on my own. I'll just watch here for a few more minutes. Call you later, Hertha. Hopefully we'll both have good news by then."

But after the couple left, Eve had a hard time tearing her eyes away from the monitors. She was still there half an hour later when the loudspeaker blared once more.

"All personnel involved with the linking experiment, go to your stations. There has been no damage to our equipment... phone lines are working here, so the test will go on as scheduled. Repeat, we are a Go for testing Project LinkUp. And if successful, we will stay on line and use the new interface to help reestablish worldwide communications with the San Francisco Bay area."

A cheer went up around the room. Eve watched as, one by one, the monitors shifted from earthquake coverage to rows of streaming numbers. The countdown clocks came alive. Five minutes till Project LinkUp.

Almost mesmerized, she mentally counted as the numbers ran down. Then shaking her head, she turned and left the room. She would try to contact Janet from home.

Remembering she had stowed her purse and shawl in her desk drawer, Eve walked through the white-tiled corridors behind the testing labs as fast as her high heels allowed. Somehow, the countdown continued in her head.

With heels clicking on the shiny hallway floor, she found herself chanting the numbers.

"Ten, nine, eight . . . three, two, one. Oh, Lord!"

A deep rumbling vibration ran through every muscle in Eve's body. The floor heaved and she felt her feet go out from under her.

It's another earthquake . . . maybe stronger than the first, she thought analytically, even as she fell—head-first—toward the sharp corner molding where the two corridors met.

Pain. Lights. First red, then blue. Then a swirling black dot appeared, which grew and grew until it swallowed up the wall, the corridor . . . and finally, Eve.

A word tore out of her throat in the last instant before her mind fell into that ebony whirlpool of un-imaginable forces. One word. A shout, a name.

"Sam!"

Chapter Three

"Sam!"

His name echoed around the white-tiled hallway. Sam's eyes jerked up from the report he had been reading in time to see Eve trip and start to fall. Dropping the booklet, he desperately lunged forward. His fingertips grazed her suit jacket, but it was too late. She careened headfirst into the corner where two corridors joined.

"Oh, God, Eve! Are you all right?" Falling to his knees when she didn't answer, Sam made a quick assessment of her condition.

He could see she had knocked herself unconscious, but there was no obvious bleeding. When his fingers found the pulse below her ear, it felt strong and steady.

"Eve, please open your eyes."

A groan, then her lids flickered open. Her deep green irises seemed empty at first. But a second later they focused on him with sharp awareness.

"Wh-where ... What ... What hap— S-Sam?" she asked thickly, seemingly not in complete control of her tongue.

"Got it right in one, Eve. Don't worry, you're going to be fine. Here, let me see if your head's bleeding. You really whacked it falling into the corner."

Sam gently probed Eve's hair. Thick and soft, he couldn't remember ever touching anything quite so silky as these sun-tipped blond strands.

"Ouch!" She flinched.

"Right here?" he soothed, carefully making a part to reveal a small gash. Blood still oozed from the cut. Sam pulled out a fresh handkerchief from his pocket and pressed it against the wound.

"That hurts, Sam," Eve complained, pulling slightly away. She looked up at him, puzzlement drawing a line between her finely arched brows.

"It's not bad," he assured her after examining the small amount of blood on the cloth and then touching her temple just below the cut. "You were lucky. If you had hit your head a little lower, it might have been more serious."

And if I had been just a little quicker, this might not have happened at all to Eve. Shaking his head to dispel images of "what might have been," Sam forcefully reminded himself that he had finished with that kind of thinking.

Living meant making constant decisions. Like what shirt to wear in the morning, or whether to turn on the radio while driving to work. Right now he had to decide whether or not to stroke Eve's face and calm the sudden anxiety he saw flare in her eyes.

Sam found the choice already made when his hand reached out and a finger traced Eve's high, Slaviclike cheekbone. Her skin felt smooth to his touch. And so did her finely fashioned, stubborn chin. He didn't dare touch her full, ripe lips.

Fighting not to groan out loud, Sam forced himself to move a few inches back from Eve. He focused all of his attention on folding his hankie and jamming it back into one pocket, then picking up the fallen report and sticking it in another. It only took a second more to regain firm control.

"Eve, do you think you can get up?" he asked, ready to help her if necessary.

"I think so." She got to her knees in a graceful rolling motion, but when she tried to use her right foot to rise further, she almost fell over.

"Is your ankle hurt?" Sam demanded, easing her back into a sitting position.

"No, it's my shoe...the heel is too short," she said, examining the pump. Her eyes met his. The helpless, beseeching expression undid him.

Just feeling, not thinking, Sam took her mouth. Incredibly, her soft, soft lips offered not the least bit of resistance to the light kiss he brushed on them. He felt her arms curl around his neck, her firm, full breasts press hard into his chest.

Sweet! Oh, so sweet. A month of wanting, a month of frustration. He had never tasted anything so heady as the honeyed nectar of her mouth.

"Oh! Oh, my Lord," Eve suddenly protested, pushing him away.

Sam groaned, damning himself for what he had just done. How could he forget her injury? How could he forget his priorities?

"I'm sorry, Eve. Let's get you to the clinic and have the doctor look at that cut."

Sam leaned over and scooped Eve into his arms. Standing upright, he strode the short distance to the facility's infirmary, passing a few wide-eyed people on the way.

Eve had struggled in his grasp for a second, but then, with a sound somewhere between a groan and a sigh, she rested her cheek against his shoulder.

The wave of rightness cresting within Sam almost overwhelmed him. Eve was finally in his arms, though not in the way he had fantasized for the past few weeks. He had wanted her from the moment he'd first met her, almost a month ago. And the more he saw of Eve, the more he got to know her, the deeper the ache had become.

She was everything he desired in a woman—smart, independent, and funny—tall and generously built. He hadn't experienced anything like this since the first rush of passion he had felt for Amber. But that had happened more than four years ago. He remembered those times fondly, but they were gone, and he had given up on ever finding that kind of emotion again.

Yet, of all the women he had known before and after marrying Amber, he had never encountered this depth of need or longing. And now, at the first real opportunity to show Eve how he felt, he had taken advantage of her weakness. It was not how he wanted to start a relationship with her. Oh, he wanted her desire, he wanted to unlock the passion he sensed in her, but only when the time was right. Only when she trusted him enough to open up, to drop the barriers she had put between them almost from the first day they'd met.

Reaching the clinic, he pushed through the double doors. "There's been an accident, get the doctor," he demanded of the receptionist at the desk. The young woman immediately jumped up at his bark of command and hurried down a short hallway.

A second later Dennis Hartcourt rushed out of his inner office.

"Is that Eve? Here, put her right down," the physician directed Sam, pulling aside a curtain hiding an examination table.

Sam wasn't happy it was this sandy-haired medic on duty. He knew the doctor and Eve had been dating. Julie Rosen had filled him in. And remembering the conversation, Sam couldn't suppress a humorous quirk of his mouth.

The head of The Monterey Yenta Association had pumped him with all the expertise of a world-class interrogator. While he hadn't told the inquisitive redhead anything he didn't want her to know, it was only because he had been trained so well to hold back vital information.

"Eve, what's the problem?" Dennis asked. He moved to her side, and indicated with a wave of his hand that Sam should go.

Sam stepped back a bit, but no way was he going to leave Eve alone with this guy.

"My head...it hurts," she began. "There were lights, and then the black whirlpool. I—I don't know why..."

"She fell and hit the right side of her head against a corner molding," Sam supplied.

"Yes, yes, I did," Eve confirmed. "I remember now. I was on the way to my office. I wanted to try to call my sister from that phone, because they wouldn't let us do it in the communications room. There was a strong aftershock, and I tripped on my high heels."

"Aftershock?" Dennis asked, probing her head with expert fingers.

"Ouch! That's it," Eve confirmed.

Sam couldn't help wincing at her pain and confusion. But the doctor only continued his examination, separating strands of hair for a better look at the wound.

"What aftershock was that?" Dennis murmured, sounding a bit distracted while he concentrated on her injury.

"From the big earthquake…an hour ago. You were in…the cafeteria when it happened…with Tawny, I think…" Eve went on, muttering disjointedly.

Dennis looked up from where he had been cleaning the area with a swab and antiseptic. Over Eve's gleaming blond head, Sam engaged in a quizzical communication with Hartcourt. It seemed that she might be more affected by the fall than he had at first thought.

"Okay, the bleeding's stopped. I don't think any stitches are needed. I've snipped a little hair, and put on butterfly bandages to keep the edges of the cut together. Now, Eve, follow the light with your eyes… No, don't look at Sam…don't move your head at all."

After her darting glance his way that caused a strange jolt in the region of his heart, Sam watched while Dennis put Eve through a series of visual exercises with a penlight.

"Good…good. Can you tell me your full name?"

"Name? Oh, I see. Eve Anne Gray."

"And how old are you, Eve?"

"Twenty-three, almost twenty-four."

Sam's eyes widened a fraction. He had thought she was older…closer to thirty. She had such an aura of calm maturity about her. What else didn't he know about her? Why didn't Eve want him to get closer to her?

"Now, can you count backward by sevens, starting with a hundred?"

"A hundred, ninety-three, eighty-six, seventy-nine..."

Sam found himself smiling while Eve rattled off the correct number sequence. He didn't think *he* could have done so well, and he hadn't just butted his head against a wall.

"Great, Eve. You're tracking fine, your pupils are equally reactive, and that bit of disorientation seems to have cleared up. I don't think there's a need for an X ray, let alone a CAT scan. But you might have a humdinger of a headache for a day or so. Be careful when you wash or comb your hair. You can hide the butterflies by arranging the strands over them. If they come off, or you have any more bleeding, call me, or see your regular doctor. Is your tetanus immunization up to date?"

"Up to date? What do you mean?"

"Have you had a shot in the last ten years?" Dennis clarified for her.

"Oh...yes. About five years ago."

"Good." Hartcourt walked to a cabinet and extracted a couple of pills. Filling a paper cup with water, he handed it to Eve.

"Take these aspirin right now, and then a couple more every four hours for pain and to reduce any swelling. I suggest you go home and get some sleep. But don't drive yourself. Also, somebody should be there to wake you up every couple of hours in the next four. They should also check your reactions. Is there anybody at home who can do that for you?''

Eve just looked at him, not seeming to understand the question. But then she blinked and answered. "No...there's nobody at all at home."

Something in her voice made Sam want to cross the room and take her in his arms.

But before he could move, the doctor glanced at his watch and announced, "Well, I'm off duty in a little bit. If you want to wait until my replacement comes in, I can take you home and stay for a while."

"No, I'm going to drive her! I know how to look for signs of concussion," Sam broke in. Even he was surprised by the deadly harshness of his words.

As if reacting to that force, Eve tried to get up. Sam immediately moved to her side, helping her to sit upright.

"It won't be necessary for either of you to drive me home," she said firmly, shrugging away from his touch. "I'm feeling a lot better, Dennis...Sam. See."

Sam watched as Eve purposefully slid off the table. She immediately grabbed on to its edge, looking like she had found the floor a lot farther away than it should have been. Eve lifted one foot, and again examined her pump as if she had never seen it before. Muttering to herself, she plucked at the material of her suit jacket.

The dazed expression in her eyes when she looked over at Sam instantly galvanized him.

"No more arguments, Eve, I'm taking you home," he informed her with all the steel he could put into his tone.

Beautiful green eyes searched his face. But instead of the protest he had expected, Eve just nodded her acceptance of his help. Good! One giant step forward.

"Thanks for all you've done for me, Dennis," Eve said, glancing over her shoulder before Sam guided her out of the cubicle.

Following them into the waiting room, the doctor called out just as they got to the exit, "I'm sure you'll be feeling much better by tomorrow, Eve, and by Friday we'll be able to dance up a storm."

"Friday? What do you mean—"

Not wanting to hear any more about Dennis's expectations for Friday evening, Sam had Eve through the door before the two could exchange another word. He immediately felt remorseful at the wave of bewilderment he saw surge into her eyes.

Dammit, he had no business playing caveman games with her in this condition.

"The parking lot's only a few steps down this hallway," he reminded Eve, gently squeezing her shoulders with his supporting hand.

"But I have to get my purse and shawl from my office," she protested. "They're in my desk drawer, along with my house and car keys. And what about my car? I can't just leave it . . ."

"Don't worry, it'll be all right. Remember, the lot is guarded twenty-four hours a day." *And leaving it here will give me the excuse to pick you up in the morning,* Sam thought, suddenly pleased with at least this turn of events. The more time he had alone with her, the better his chances. "I'll go get your stuff from your office in a minute, but first I'm taking you to my car."

Perhaps realizing how shaken she still was, Eve gave in with a wave of her hand toward the nearby door.

A blast of bright sunshine buffeted them when they exited the windowless building. Eve gave a sudden moan and squeezed her eyes shut, as if she couldn't deal with the glare.

"Hi, Ms. Gray, Mr. Davidson. What's wrong?" the young African-American marine guarding the door asked when he saw Sam supporting Eve.

"She's had a minor accident, Corporal Bishop. I'll be driving her home, so her car will be here overnight," Sam informed the man, and then guided Eve to his nearby green Chevy.

Eve didn't open her eyes until Sam got her into the passenger seat.

"It's daytime," she murmured, her confusion evident by the wobble of her voice. "How long was I unconscious, Sam?"

"Just a minute or two," he quickly assured her. "Don't worry, Eve. It's going to be all right. Here, I'll roll down the window. You just sit still while I get your stuff. Be back in a flash."

EVE WATCHED Sam's long-legged stride quickly take him into the building. She briefly shut her eyes once more as confusion swirled around her, but then forced them open to face reality.

Looking down at her feet, she confirmed what she had seen in the clinic. Instead of her green pumps, she now wore the shoes she favored for her long work days, which were black, and an inch-and-a-half shorter. She was also wearing her gray wool work suit, not her green silk cocktail dress.

When had she changed clothes? What could have happened to her to make her forget doing that? Of course, she knew she had hit her head. Everyone agreed on that much. But what about the rest? Why was it daytime, instead of just after midnight? And why hadn't Sam or Dennis seemed concerned about the devastating earthquake that had just happened?

In fact, when she'd mentioned the aftershock had caused her to trip, a sudden silence had fallen between the men. And now that her mind felt a little clearer, Eve recalled a worried look passing between them.

What was going on? Her brain was full of memories of the most horrible sort. In her mind's eye she could still see the live television feed that had panned Berkeley, showing collapsed buildings, overturned freeways, and people wandering around in shock.

And yet both Sam and Dennis were as cool as clichéd cucumbers about an event that couldn't have taken place more than an hour ago.

An hour ago? No, that was wrong. Eve looked out the window again and found herself squinting in the bright, slanting sunlight. The quake had happened at eleven at night, the aftershock at about twelve. But now, the angle of the December sun warming her face said it had to be around four in the afternoon.

Yet, Sam said she had been unconscious for only a minute or so. Sam!

"Oh, my Lord, he kissed me!" Eve's anguished moan bounced around the interior of the car.

How could he have done that? How could she have let him? And why had he even been in the corridor when she fell? Eve distinctly remembered seeing him leave with Amber, obviously on their way home right after the first quake.

Perhaps he had come back as soon as he had made sure Amber was safely in their apartment. But, no, that wasn't right...she had forgotten again that the aftershock happened at midnight, and it was now broad daylight.

Leaning back against the headrest, Eve fought off a rising sense of panic by once again trying to order her thoughts.

First of all, she had fallen and hit her head. Second, it was no longer midnight on New Year's Eve. In fact, looking around the parking lot, she saw it was filled, as if this were an ordinary workday and not the Saturday following the party. So today had to be at least Monday...no, Tuesday. Monday was a government holiday, to make up for New Year's Day falling on Saturday.

Obviously she was missing almost four days from her memory. Somehow the fall on New Year's Eve had caused amnesia. And she must have tripped again, half an hour ago, which jogged her brain back to normal.

Scary, but she could live with that, she decided, taking a deep breath and once again closing her eyes. Instantly a vision of herself in Sam's arms, his mouth tenderly closing on hers—the taste of him, the scent of him—assailed Eve.

No! That could not have happened. It went against everything she knew about Sam. He was completely devoted to his wife.

"I must have imagined that kiss, because of the blow to my head," Eve forcefully told herself. And then sighed. Because, imagined or not, it had been so sweet.

Eve jumped in guilty panic when the driver's side door abruptly opened.

"Here you go," Sam said, handing over the large brown leather purse he had retrieved for her. "I couldn't find a shawl. Check your handbag to see if anything else is missing."

Trying to recover her poise, Eve made a quick appraisal of her purse. "No, no, there's nothing gone. And I guess I didn't bring my shawl to work...today."

"Well, okay. But, you know, it isn't a good idea to keep valuables in an unlocked desk drawer. Anyone could walk in, like I just did, and waltz out with them."

"Spoken like a true security person," Eve countered with a shaky smile. "Not that I don't understand what you're saying. But in the year and a half I've worked here, I've never heard of anything being stolen."

"Then all of you have been lucky," Sam said, adding one of his gorgeous grins before he started the ignition and rolled down his window.

"Your other car being serviced?" Eve asked, trying to cancel out the immediate effect his smile had on her by saying the first thing that came to mind.

"Other car?"

"Yes. The one you usually drive to work, the dark blue station wagon with the automatic windows."

The one I first saw you in when we shared our Mozart musical moment in the Safeway parking lot, Eve wanted to say, but didn't. She didn't dare reinforce that stupid refrain, if by some chance Sam had managed to forget it.

"A blue station... Hey, look out, you fool!" Sam suddenly shouted out the window. He managed to brake in time to avoid colliding with a pickup truck changing lanes without signaling. "Sorry about that.

It was partly my fault for not paying closer attention. Did that quick stop jolt your head?"

"No, I don't think so. I didn't notice any pain, anyway."

Sam nodded and then concentrated on the traffic when they started again. Eve couldn't help noticing the sheen of perspiration dotting his wide forehead. Odd, in the cool December air. *No, not December, we're into January,* she reminded herself.

What had she missed in the past few days? How bad had that quake really been? And were Janet and Steven all right? She wondered if they had contacted her... or if she had called them.

Lord, she had a hundred questions, but whom should she ask? Sam? No, just sitting next to him in this confined space was sheer torture for Eve. She had to get away from him—to erase the memory of that imagined kiss—as quickly as possible.

Julie! Julie would know what had happened to her since the New Year's Eve party. And surely there would be clues at home. The newspapers, television reports—something to fill in the disconcerting void in her memory. Maybe she should go back and tell Dennis about this mental lapse she had discovered...

"So, now I know you've been working at the facility for eighteen months," Sam said, breaking into Eve's churning thoughts. "You never told me that fact in any of the coffee breaks we've shared. Is this your first government job?"

Happy to be able to tell him something she had no trouble remembering, Eve divulged more to Sam than she ordinarily would have done.

"My first real job, period. I got it right out of college, when I was recruited by the Federal Scholar's program."

"Scholar…hmm? Impressive. Where did you go to school?"

"U.C., Berkeley."

"Berkeley? Hey, my best friend from college, Dave Sutter, teaches up there. Ever take any geology classes?"

"No. I did a double major in math and statistics. So I tried to take the few electives I had in the humanities, mostly music."

As usual, thinking about her career decision made Eve remember how unhappy her parents had been with her choice. They had desperately wanted her to accept the scholarship to Juilliard, where she could study with the best piano teachers and begin concertizing.

Lost in her memories, it took a few minutes for Eve to realize they had passed through Monterey and were now within the boundaries of Pacific Grove. And she didn't remember giving Sam her address, or directions. How did he know she lived here? Had he gone through her purse?

"You'll have to tell me where to go from here," he said, almost as if reading the accusation in her mind.

"But how did you know I lived in Pacific Grove?" she challenged. Was that a flush of red rising under his deeply tanned skin?

"Uh, I must have heard someone say something. Can't remember, exactly. Mind's like a sieve sometimes. But I've heard *you* have a trick memory…photographic," he said.

Although Eve knew that Sam had just changed the subject, she found herself answering him. "Actually, it's eidetic. Which means that if I concentrate hard on recalling a past event, I remember everything I've seen, read, heard or thought. It can be a real bummer," she muttered.

"Yeah, I can understand what you mean. Great for history classes, but hell when you *want* to forget something."

Something in Sam's voice made Eve feel as though he really did understand what it was like to relive a traumatic event in exact detail, over and over again. She remembered his words at the New Year's party, telling Amber that she shouldn't dance because her *latest* operation had only been three months earlier. Was he remembering Amber's pain? Whatever they had gone through must have been horrendous.

The thought of their past agony touched some deep recess in Eve's heart. And looking inside herself, she discovered this sense of empathy resided right next to her feelings for Sam...the unwanted obsession she had thought vanquished.

Damn! It was no use. Even meeting Amber hadn't helped her. Eve finally admitted she was doomed to desire this man until the day she died.

What a mess!

She shook her head, and then wished she hadn't when a stabbing pain sliced through her temple. Trying not to gasp out loud, she took deep breaths until the spasm receded.

After giving Sam final instructions on how to get to her house, she closed her eyes. He seemed content with the silence that fell between them. It lasted until they pulled up in front of her house.

SAM GUIDED THE CAR to a stop. He was about to announce their arrival when he noticed Eve's eyes were closed. Which was good, because she needed the rest, and he needed a minute to make sure his cheeks had stopped glowing.

Wow, when was the last time he had blushed?

Probably about the same year he had his first mad crush—on Mary Ann O'Malley—who had sat in front of him in his eighth-grade English class at Munger Junior High.

Every chance he got, he would tool his bike along the tidy, westside Detroit streets, past Mary Ann's two-storied brick house, just on the off chance he might catch a glimpse of her.

Obsessed. He had been absolutely crazy about that girl. Probably because she was out of bounds. Even in that lower-class neighborhood, there were strata. And he literally lived on the other side of the railroad tracks.

The Davidson family was relegated to occupying a second-floor flat in a sagging, run-down rental house. Mostly because his father drank away the good money he made on the auto assembly line.

And even though I don't live by the railroad tracks anymore, Eve has placed herself out of bounds, too, Sam thought. Oh, she was friendly enough at work. They'd shared coffee breaks a score of times in the last few weeks…because he'd engineered them. During the public tête-à-têtes, they discussed a dozen topics of mutual interest. Yet she'd put up this insurmountable barrier, almost from the day they had met. "Thus far, and no further," was the message her body language blared.

Sam could have taken her refusal to respond and left her alone. He wasn't God's gift to women, and his attentions had been turned down before. But he had seen a look in her eyes, a longing that made Sam certain Eve was fighting the same attraction he felt...and God knew he had never experienced anything this strong before. Even with Amber...poor Amber.

Sam closed his eyes and tried to drive away the memory of how he had betrayed his wife in the past...and in the present. This obsession for Eve often pushed Amber completely out of his thoughts.

Obsession. For the past few weeks Sam had been reliving his youth. He had looked up Eve's address and often driven past this lovely house late at night when he couldn't sleep. And when he needed to get out of that tiny apartment, away from his midnight regrets about Amber.

Each time he came by, he hoped to get a glimpse of Eve, even her shadow, through the blinds covering the wide lower windows.

Under the red-tiled roof, the upper-story windows didn't seem to have blinds or drapes. A...veranda, he guessed it was called in this part of the country, ran the length of the top floor. The sea must be visible from up there. The view would be beautiful.

Sam turned his gaze from the house to Eve.

"Beautiful," he murmured out loud.

"Yes, it is a wonderful house," Eve surprised Sam by responding, after opening her eyes and looking around. "One of the few Monterey-style adobes here in Pacific Grove. Not that the Victorian era houses aren't gorgeous. 'Painted ladies' all dressed up in their gingerbread finery." She pointed to the colorful neighboring homes.

Ending the short architecture lesson abruptly, Eve reached over to push open the passenger door... only to turn back to Sam.

She gazed at him for several aching heartbeats, as if trying to decide something monumental. He found he was holding his breath in anticipation.

"Sam..." she finally began. "Sam, I—I have to ask you. Tell me...was there a major earthquake up north on the Hayward Fault within the past few days?"

It certainly wasn't what he had expected her to say! But just what *had* he expected? An invitation into her home? A demand that he kiss her senseless? A declaration of love?

Shaking his head, Sam felt a wry grin stretch his mouth. "No, Eve, no quake anywhere up there. At least nothing big for the last seven years or so."

"But it seemed so real. Lord, it *still* feels so real!" Eve rubbed her head. Then with a quick "Thanks for driving me home, Sam," she was out of the car and halfway up the red brick path before he could catch her.

"Whoa, Eve. Don't rush like this."

"I'm all right, really," she assured him, stopping at the weathered oak front door. Fumbling in her purse, she produced a set of keys, which promptly fell out of her fingers.

Swiftly retrieving them, Sam ignored her protests and unlocked the wide door himself. Holding on to Eve's elbow, he guided her through the short vestibule, which led into a large living room.

The inviting smell of baked goods and pine needles enticed his nose.

"Just put the keys on top of my purse, here on this end table," Eve directed, pulling away from him and tossing her handbag on the floor as she crossed the shadowy room. She bumped her leg against the edge of a coffee table when she reached the other side.

"Damn, I've turned into a first-class klutz," Sam heard her mutter. Continuing in a louder voice, she made for a hallway. "I'm going to take a couple more aspirin and then lay down, Sam. Would you just close the front door on your way out? It's self-locking. Thanks again for everything. See you at work tomorrow."

Restraining the impulse to follow her into what must be a first-floor bedroom, Sam stopped at the door she had just closed. He identified the sound of running water, then the opening of a dresser drawer. The swishing plop of clothing puddling to the floor provoked a mental image of Eve's tall, lush body, with bare skin gleaming palely in the winter afternoon light.

Feeling like a randy voyeur, he nevertheless waited at her door until the sigh of a mattress signaled she was safely in bed.

Walking back into the living room, he picked up her purse and put it, along with her keys, on the only end table he could find. It was located near an enormous fireplace, several feet away from where Eve had dropped her handbag.

Wandering around, Sam examined the many pictures and tapestries hanging on the walls. At a floor-to-ceiling bookcase, he checked out some of the titles.

Along with a whole slew of mathematics texts and music tapes, there were rows of science fiction classics. With his index finger, he traced the spines of some of his favorites: *The Man in the High Castle, The Lincoln Hunters, The City and the Stars* and a complete set of Robert Heinlein's books, even his early juveniles.

He remembered Eve saying during coffee one day that she was addicted to speculative fiction, just as he was. Even so, he was surprised by how many of the same novels they both owned.

He had acquired most of his collection in college, but he had been reading the genre since he was a skinny, little kid of twelve or so. Not able to buy them in those days, every week he would borrow a backpackful of science fiction from the neighborhood library.

Each night, Sam had dived into the books, using the engrossing stories to help shut out the sounds of his father's rages and his mother's pleadings.

Abruptly turning away from the memory, Sam moved to the left of the bookcases, walking into a deep alcove in which a graceful Christmas tree flanked a concert grand piano. Searching for a minute, he gave in to the impulse to switch on the electricity. Softly colored lights instantly turned the area into a multicolored grotto.

The illumination gleaming on the piano also revealed a small bookcase, filled with sheet music and bound scores. Examining a particularly thick volume, Sam found it was a "cheat book," containing the melody lines for hundreds of the most popular songs from the past fifty or sixty years. He knew professional musicians used these to play audience requests.

Bemused, Sam went back to the living room bookcases. Without thinking about the liberties he was taking, he picked out a volume at random, slipped Mozart's forty-second symphony—"The Redemption''—into the tape deck, and then sat down in a comfortable easy chair.

After setting his watch alarm to activate in two hours, so he could wake Eve up on time, he began reading the book he had chosen. Only then did Sam discover Eve owned a copy of Sarban's *The Sound of His Horn*, perhaps his most beloved story of that particular subgenre. It seemed like a wonderful portent about their possible future together.

Maybe it was the book, or the Christmas tree, or the emotional music playing softly in the richness of this superb room . . . but whatever the reason, Sam hadn't felt this good—this at peace—since the day he'd married Amber.

Chapter Four

"Eve. Wake up, Eve!"

It was the voice, deep and husky, that led her out of the dark dream. Somehow she knew the owner of this voice could help her vanquish the *bête noire* in which she ran down a maze of unfamiliar streets, where buildings tilted overhead at crazy angles and the sky between them glowed with a strange, actinic light.

"Eve? Are you all right? You were crying, sweetheart. It sounded like you were having a horrible nightmare."

Tell me about it! she thought with a shiver of remembrance. Her eyes opened and then focused on Sam. *And now I'm having an erotic fantasy.* One in which Sam Davidson sat on the edge of her bed, his wide shoulders blocking out the rest of the room, his gentle fingers wiping away tears from her cheeks.

It was such a realistic fantasy that when she reached out to touch his face, she felt the rough scrape of the dark whiskers shadowing his firm chin and lean cheeks.

And as in all her dreams of Sam, she raised open arms, waiting—longing—to be swept up into his strong, enveloping embrace.

But the arms closing around her this time—the arms lifting her from the pillow and pulling her near—were no midnight abstraction. They bulged with thick, heavy muscles. The skin covering them felt warmly alive, almost hot. And the wide chest she pressed against had absolutely nothing in common with her squishy down-filled pillow.

"Sam?" Eve suddenly pushed away from him... from the realization that he actually *was* in her bedroom. "What are you doing? Why are you here?" He should have gone home... to Amber.

"It's time," Sam said, pointing to his wristwatch.

"Time?" What time was it? What *day* was it! Unable to focus on the watch dial in the lamp's dim light, Eve looked for the digital readout of her bedside clock.

Looked, but didn't find. Because her clock was gone. Why the missing timepiece should bother her so much seemed strange—especially when she compared it to having Sam Davidson on her bed! But illogical or not, Eve's gaze bounced wildly around the room, frantically searching until she finally located the clock. It's glowing numbers seemed to hover a short distance over the mirrored dresser, next to the window.

It was 7:05 p.m. She had been asleep about two hours.

"You moved my clock!" she accused peevishly. "Did I give you permission to move my clock?"

Sam looked over to where she was pointing. "No, sweetheart, it was there when I came in to wake you. Is your head hurting... are you seeing double?"

Moving her head slowly back and forth, Eve stared up at Sam in confusion. Double? She couldn't even cope with *one* of him! The desire to have him take her in his arms again was almost overwhelming.

With the preservation of her dignity—and her secret desires—in mind, Eve scooted back from Sam, trying to pull the quilt up like a shield.

"Why are you here?" she demanded again.

"As I said before, it's time to check you out, darling." A wide grin stretched his mouth at the sound of her loud gasp.

"Check me out?" she echoed stupidly.

"To make sure you don't have any lingering effects from that crack on your head, sweetheart" he clarified, reaching out his long fingers to touch her temple.

"Stop doing that."

"Stop touching you, darling?" he murmured.

"No. Yes! I mean, stop doing *everything*. Touching me, calling me sweetheart ... darling. What's gotten into you, Sam?" Eve protested.

As if the panic in her voice had finally reached him, his wonderful grin faded.

"I'm sorry, Eve. I didn't mean to take advantage of the situation and tease. But I do need to have a good look at you."

When *that* statement made her pull back even farther against the headboard, the quilt slipped, momentarily revealing the full swell of her breasts in the scooped neckline of her nightie.

"Oh, boy! Be careful what you wish for, Davidson," Sam muttered, abruptly getting off the bed and crossing the room. He stopped at the entryway, his gaze fixed on the door. "Eve, put on some more clothes, a robe—something—and then come out where the light's better. Don't worry, I'm just going to examine your eyes. I swear."

At the sound of the door clicking shut on that strangely fervent vow, Eve swung her feet off the bed. Throwing on a sweatshirt and jeans in record time, she carefully brushed out her hair, avoiding the area around the wound. Then using a scarf, she tied the thick, long mass at the nape of her neck. After pushing her narrow feet into a pair of moccasin loafers, she took a big breath and went out into the hall.

Entering the living room, she bumped into the coffee table. It had somehow gotten moved halfway across the floor. A book lay open on it, a coffee cup resting on a coaster sat nearby. Music—Mozart?—played softly from the tape deck speakers, only to click off at that moment.

"Certainly made himself right at home," she muttered, then, raising her voice, "Sam? Sam, where are you?"

"In the kitchen. Come on in."

Mouthing a string of mild expletives at his invitation to enter her own kitchen, Eve crossed the room and pushed open the swinging doors separating the two areas.

The smell of freshly brewed coffee made her mouth water. On the table, two places were set. Sam's suit jacket hung on the back of one chair. He stood at the stove, cutting a steaming, golden omelet in two with a spatula.

"Dinner is almost ready. I just have to make the toast. Sit down and read the newspaper. Your carrier delivered it about an hour ago," he said, indicating the folded afternoon edition resting on the table.

Maybe because she suddenly realized she was ravenous, Eve obediently sat down as he suggested and picked up the paper. But then she put it down again. The sight of this tall man in her kitchen, efficiently organizing a meal as if he did it every day, was too compelling for any other distraction.

A minute later Sam slid a plate with half the omelet and a side of sourdough toast in front of her. After pouring Eve a cup of coffee, he took his seat and then waited for her reaction to the eggs with a raised black eyebrow.

"Wonderful," she said around the first mouthful. "This is the best cheese omelet I've ever eaten."

"You don't have to sound so surprised. I do know my way around the kitchen. Hard to reach thirty-two without learning to fend for oneself," he said with a wry grin, and then tucked into his own plate.

Of course, Sam would know how to cook, Eve considered while she demolished her serving. And he certainly knew how to shop, remembering his Safeway outing. He could probably wash clothes and clean, too, because of Amber's fragile condition.

Even if he could afford regular domestic help, he must have to do more than his share of the household duties. Evidently, Amber had gone through a series of operations in the past few years, and only now had recovered enough to resume normal activities.

Resume normal activities? *Oh, dear Lord,* Eve mentally gasped. *What if Sam and Amber haven't been able to...* Eve's hand began to shake so hard she was forced to put down her coffee cup.

Sam *had* used endearments in the bedroom. And he'd held her far closer than was necessary to comfort her...almost as tightly as Eve had desired. And had she really imagined that sweetly searing kiss this afternoon in the hallway of the facility?

What if all of this sudden, intense attention was the result of a long period of sexual frustration on his part? A picture of Sam dancing with Amber at the New Year's party flashed into Eve's mind.

She remembered the strangely intense look he had given her. What if after years of denial, Sam had finally reached the limit of his endurance? Perhaps he wanted Eve to stand in for Amber in those areas where his wife couldn't—

No! Never!

"Well, that was delicious. Th-thanks, S-Sam," Eve said in a voice as shaky as her hand. Scooping up her plate and cup, she took them over to the sink. "You should go home, now. Hope the dinner waiting for you can be saved. I forgot to ask, did you call . . ."

She had taken only a couple of steps toward the living room door before Sam reached her side and effectively cut off her question—and her escape—in midsyllable.

"I'm in no hurry to get home," he interrupted, smiling down on her.

His crooked grin almost did her in. Feeling her resolve to get him out of her house as quickly as possible begin to crumble, Eve shook her head, hard. A serious mistake. The stab of pain she felt made her gasp. The room spun alarmingly and she staggered.

Sam instantly grabbed her shoulders and sat her down on a chair.

"You stay there. I'm going to examine your eyes, right now. Do you have a flashlight?"

Rubbing her head, Eve pointed to the top of the refrigerator, where she kept a few votive candles and a flashlight in case of power outages.

Sam strode over and grabbed the device. Back at the table, he tilted Eve's chin up. She couldn't help flinching at his touch.

"Just going to take a quick look at your eye reflexes," he said soothingly, as if he were trying to tame a skittish colt. His own eyes had narrowed to fierce slits. "Open them wide, Eve. Okay, now keep looking at me."

He switched off the flashlight and quickly turned it on again.

"Good…both of your irises are reacting the same. Watch the light, but move only your eyes . . . not your head. Great. Looking good, Eve. Really lookin' good."

The last words were followed by a sweeping appraisal of Eve's face and body. And if she had felt heat emitting from him before, it was nothing compared to the laserlike intensity of the deep blue gaze that seemed to penetrate her loose sweatshirt and tight jeans.

"Yes, well, I *am* feeling much better, Sam. Again, thank you so much, for everything. I'll just see you to the door."

This time Eve managed to do an end run around the man and his fullback shoulders. She pushed through the kitchen doors into the living room, and marched to the small vestibule.

Sam followed only a few steps behind. Putting on his suit jacket as he crossed the floor, his step was surprisingly quiet on the wood planking.

"I turned out the tree lights before I woke you, but I'll just put the rest of these things back where they belong before I leave," he said, pointing to the open book and coffee cup on the misplaced table.

"Oh, don't bother with those," Eve said, not really listening in the rising surge of panic she was experiencing. She had to get him out of here before it was too late...before she made the mistake she would regret for the rest of her life.

"Hope you don't mind me reading *The Sound of His Horn*," he was saying with maddening calm. "I realize it's a first American edition, but I couldn't resist. Lost my own copy some twenty years ago. I'd forgotten how good it is."

"No problem. Here, why don't you finish it at home? Give the book back to me at work, when you're done."

Eve ran to retrieve the slim volume. Holding the novel out like a lure, she dashed to the small vestibule and threw the front door open.

Obviously puzzled by her strange antics, Sam shook his head, but finally followed her. He took the paperback from her outstretched hand and put it in his suit coat pocket.

"I'll be careful with it," he promised. "Eve, I think you should go back to bed now. I'll call in about two hours to check on you, like Dennis suggested. But from what I've seen, I think you're out of the woods and should be able to go to work in the morning. About tomorrow...I'll pick you up around seven-thirty."

"Pick me up?"

"Right, your car is still in the parking lot at work, remember?"

She remembered.

Once again she vividly recalled the fall, the blackness, the swirling void into which she had dived. Eve also remembered that she had forgotten at least four days of her life!

For someone who had been blessed—or cursed— with total recall, that gap in her memory was especially frightening.

As soon as she could get rid of Sam, she planned to read the afternoon newspaper to find out what she had missed . . . and to confirm what day it was! Then she would call Julie to learn the rest of what had happened to her during those lost days.

But while Sam stood looking down at her, she acknowledged that, even more disturbing than misplacing a few days, was the false memory of Sam's honeyed kiss in the hallway at work.

Involuntarily, Eve found herself gazing at his wide mouth. The upper lip was long and very thin; the lower one full and firm. A woman would hate having a mouth like that. Getting her lipstick to look right would be a nightmare. But on Sam, especially with that short, sexy scar, it was a mouth made to be examined, explored . . . devoured.

As if proving mind reading really was one of his hidden talents, Sam muttered with an Irish lilt in his deep voice, "And sure it would take a saint to resist kissing a beautiful mouth like this one."

Before she could move away, one of Sam's large hands reached out to gently cup the back of Eve's blond head, while the other wrapped itself around her waist. In the next instant his mouth captured hers.

Shock lasted about two seconds. After that, it was too late. Long-denied feelings kicked into overdrive, zinging the most intense surge of sensual heat through her body that Eve had ever experienced.

It was only when Sam groaned, and his huge body pressed hers against the nearby wall, that Eve felt alarms go off. Joined to him from shoulder to thigh, she felt him teeter on a crumbling edge of control.

The hand holding her head became a tender vise. His chest began moving from side to side against her breasts; the friction made her nipples tingle and swell. That sensation sent stabbing jabs of pleasure arrowing throughout her body, from her fingertips to her toes. His embrace was as devastating as she had feared it would be.

It was the primitive, almost unintelligible words of desire torn from his throat that finally dragged Eve back from the edge of disaster. She knew in another few seconds, neither Sam nor she would have the ability to end this forbidden embrace. They would be making love on the vestibule floor, with the front door wide open to the rest of the world!

With a strength born of anger and shame, Eve wrenched away from Sam. Somehow, grabbing a fistful of suit fabric, she managed to get him outside, onto the front porch.

"I thought I knew what kind of man you were, Sam," she shouted at him. "How could you do this to me? And how could you betray the woman who trusted you?"

SAM STOOD on the doorstep, too stunned to move when Eve slammed the front door shut in his face. The sound of security bolts snicking home ended the paralysis.

Anger at himself, along with a swift surge of guilt, instantly drained the passion from his body. How could he have forced himself on Eve like that? Completely forgetting about her recent injury, he had used his masculine strength to keep her in that embrace. Dammit, he had vowed never to do that to a woman. He had never behaved like his father before.

She was right...he had betrayed her trust...badly. Lord, she had been unconscious not four hours ago. Her confusion, the way she stumbled through her own house—the strange questions she had asked—were all indications that the fall had really jogged her brain.

And what had he done? Teased her, harassed her...forced her to respond to him, to make her body admit there was an overwhelming emotion linking them that could no longer be denied.

Running a shaking hand through his hair, Sam stared at the oak door in front of him. Some sixth sense told him that Eve was still there...just behind the portal.

"Eve," he called, pressing his hand against the weathered wood, willing her to answer, or to at least listen. "Eve, I'm sorry. You're right, I did take advantage of you. And I swear, it will never happen again."

And it wouldn't. He would take things slow from now on, never demanding anything Eve was unwilling to give. But one thing he could not do. He could not turn away from the passion that had finally been unleashed between them. He had felt it from the first—the realization they were meant to be together—the certainty nothing, and no one, could come between them, now that they had finally met.

Taking a deep breath, Sam talked to the woman behind the door again. "Eve, darl— Eve. You should get some rest now. Take a couple more aspirin and go back to bed. I'll call you in a few hours to make sure you're okay. And don't forget, I'm taking you to work in the morning."

"NOT UNLESS all the taxi services on the Monterey Bay peninsula go bankrupt by tomorrow, buddy," Eve muttered from her position on the vestibule's cool slate floor. And maybe not even then. *A four-mile walk to work in the fresh ocean air would probably be good for my head,* Eve thought, rubbing her throbbing temple just below the butterfly bandages.

Well, Sam was right about one thing, she decided, slowly rising to her feet when she heard his car pull away. She did need to take a couple more aspirin and get back to bed.

Reentering the dimly lit living room, Eve crossed the floor on the way to her bedroom, this time remembering to avoid the coffee table Sam had moved.

She stopped to look at the table, and then around the whole area. With his overwhelming presence gone, Eve realized the table was not the only piece of furniture out of place.

"Damn him! It looks like he's rearranged everything. The nerve of the man!"

The couch, and adjacent end table, now sat in front of the fireplace, with the television placed for viewing nearby. Sam had also shifted her father's recliner to the position it had once occupied close to the bookshelves and stereo equipment. The coffee table was conveniently situated by the chair, just as it had been before her parents were killed.

In fact, now that she looked closer...the whole room was just as her parents had arranged it. A prickle of unease ran down Eve's back as she sniffed the air and identified the scent that had been masked by the rich coffee Sam had brewed for dinner.

Pine.

What had Sam said a few minutes ago, before their disastrous kiss? "I turned the tree lights off before waking you." Her trick memory provided his words, verbatim.

Even though she knew what to expect, when Eve slowly turned toward the alcove and saw the decorated Christmas tree, she almost lost it.

Falling into the recliner, she lowered her head between her knees and commanded her lungs to take slow, deep breaths.

One. Two. Three... The blackness receded and Eve forced herself upright once more. Getting out of the chair, she steeled her resolve to walk into the alcove and reach behind the tree; unerringly she located the light switch.

Instantly the space filled with magic...the beloved memories of her childhood were all there. Every ornament the Gray family had acquired over the years hung in its traditional arrangement on the gracefully sloping tree branches.

But each glass bulb, every silver icicle, should still be packed away on a shelf in the second-floor storage area, because she had not taken them out this year.

What else had been done to this room? Her eyes were immediately drawn to the fireplace and the stockings hanging from the oak mantel. Slowly walking over to it, Eve's hand went out to smooth down the monogrammed red stockings her mother had knitted for each member of the family. Although empty, they hung in their accustomed places.

Except for Janet's and the new one her mom had made for Steven, just before her parents' plane crash.

"Sam could not have done this," Eve declared to the dark shadows that skirted the edges of the room. Where would he have gotten a tree at this late date? How could he have known where to find the ornaments upstairs, and then hang them in just the right way?

Eve felt the beginnings of fear, like cold fingers, skittle up her spine. Her gaze darted around the room, but found no reassurance. Everything was so familiar, yet altered in a subtle, surrealistic way. Her eyes finally locked on the row of Christmas cards arranged along the mantelpiece, intermixed with her family's pictures.

Among the greetings from her friends and co-workers, one card now stood out. It was much larger than the rest, and obviously hand-painted. There was a white dove on the front, with an olive branch clutched in its beak. Wasn't that a traditional peace offering? Eve asked herself.

Picking the card up with trembling fingers, she opened it. The message penned inside had a distinctive artistic style...Janet's well-remembered handwriting.

For Eve,
We have two wishes for the New Year. Your hap-

piness and your forgiveness for all the pain we caused you.

Call us, please. On the enclosed paper, you'll find our new number and address.

With hope and love,
Janet and Steve

The card slipped from Eve's fingers back onto the mantel. Janet? Had Janet been here...and Steven? Had the card, the Christmas tree—everything—been their attempt at a reconciliation?

Running to the hallway, Eve threw open the door to the second-floor staircase. *Janet could have come this morning while I was at work,* Eve thought, taking the stairs two at a time at first, until her head protested and she slowed down.

But her thoughts still raced ahead. Janet and Steven might have moved the furniture around into the arrangement that they thought reflected happier times. And seeing she hadn't put up a tree, they could have gone out and found some plant nursery that still had one for sale.

"Janet! Janet...Steven?" she called, throwing open the door to the huge room her sister had used as a bedroom and studio.

But even as she reached for the wall switch, Eve knew the notion that they were waiting up here to surprise her was stupidly illogical.

The room was empty. Empty as it had been for a year. Every stick of furniture, each bit of equipment—every painting and drawing—had been removed a few days after her parents' funeral.

Nobody had been in here today. There were only shadows. Shadows, and the still-echoing vibrations of all that had happened after her sister had come home from Paris to attend the memorial service.

Sinking to the dusty plank floor, Eve wrapped her arms around her knees, listening to the echoes that filled her mind, remembering just why she hated her sister.

Chapter Five

Where is Janet? Eve wondered while pacing back and forth, alone in the little room the church set aside for immediate family. She checked her watch: 11:05. The funeral had been scheduled for eleven. If her sister didn't get here in the next few minutes, Janet was going to be too late for the service.

She had phoned Eve at home three hours earlier, when her flight from Paris landed in San Francisco. Janet assured her older sister that she had plenty of time to catch the commuter plane to the Monterey Peninsula Airport.

Steven had gone to pick Janet up there, well over an hour ago. Eve knew it was only a fifteen-minute trip between the airport and this Pacific Grove church. So where were they? Again checking her watch, she decided to wait five more minutes before having the minister start.

Eve gathered up her prayer book and the remembrance leaflet containing the order of service and her parents' biographies. She was about to go back into the sanctuary to speak with any latecomers when the door flew open.

It was Steven, his blond hair in windblown disarray, his tie slightly askew. However, the young woman his arm supported didn't have a thing out of place. Dressed in a pencil-thin black sheath and stiletto heels, her sable brown hair was caught up in a Psyche knot at the nape of her long, elegant neck. Her makeup—with shadow enhancing large brown eyes and blush hollowing out model-gaunt cheeks—was perfect.

"Sorry we're late," Steven said, sounding out of breath. The pained expression on his handsome face threw his chiseled features slightly out of alignment. "There was a mix-up with the luggage. But even before that... Eve, I walked right by Janet in the terminal. No one would have been able to recognize her from the description you gave me."

Janet? Steven was right, Eve would have walked by her sister, too! Gone was the plump little twenty-year-old she had seen off to Paris two years ago on an art school scholarship. In her place stood a slender, chic woman, who seemed inches taller—and was a good forty pounds lighter—than the Janet she remembered.

"Evey, I can't believe they're gone," Janet whispered from the doorway. "Dad was such a good pilot, and then... just like that... both of them dead."

Eve opened her arms and her sister rushed into them. Janet's sobs triggered the tears Eve had been fighting back all morning. Holding the smaller woman close, Eve raised wet eyes to Steven. He was at her side in an instant, his arms embracing her, and Janet.

A few minutes later he sat down between them in the front row of the sanctuary as the service began. Almost a dozen people got up to speak in loving remembrance of Warren and Patricia Gray.

But the chief eulogy, the one Eve would always remember when she thought of the funeral, was given by Father Raphael Moreno.

Taking the podium from the officiating minister, the white-haired Catholic priest looked down at Eve and Janet. The bones of his ascetic face could have been hewn from stone by an ax, but the humanity in his dark brown eyes warmed Eve as she waited for him to speak.

"We will all greatly miss Warren and Patricia," he began. "Their deaths have torn open a big hole in the fabric of our community. Warren worked tirelessly, here and in Sacramento, as a champion of the poor and the disenfranchised. As a defense attorney, he freely gave uncounted hours to seek justice for them. And when he was elected to the state legislature, he helped enact laws that will insure the continuance of his goals.

"And for me, personally, Warren Gray was a chess partner who, over the last twenty years, pushed me to the very limit of my mental capabilities and then demanded that this aging dog use his tired, old brain to learn a few more tricks and strategies."

An appreciative chuckle echoed in the sanctuary, and Eve found herself smiling through her tears at the memory of the raucous games her father and Father Moreno had played over the years.

"Patricia Gray's passing is no less a loss to our community," the priest went on. "A loving, supportive wife and mother, she also worked to pass on her knowledge of the Romance languages to our young. As a teacher of Spanish, she had no rival. She also devoted long hours working with newly arrived immigrants, acting as a compassionate bridge between them and their new neighbors.

"We can take comfort in this sad time, knowing that Patricia and Warren left us their daughters to carry on the Gray tradition."

Father Moreno stopped for a moment to look out at the mourners. He then nodded to Eve.

"In high school, Eve was a popular student, serving at various times as cheerleader, homecoming queen, and valedictorian. She earned a perfect score on her SAT exams and was offered several scholarships for her musical and mathematical abilities. And we all know that after graduating Summa Cum Laude from U.C., Berkeley, she has returned to us here to work, and to use her talents to help our community.

"Warren and Patricia were also very proud of their younger daughter, Janet. She is a promising art student, who has taken classes in Paris for the last two years."

Father Moreno paused to smile down on Eve and Janet, then with a quote from the Old Testament, gave them his blessing.

"'Many daughters have done virtuously, but thou excellest them all.' Bless you both," he said, raising his hands in benediction. "And bless us all in our time of sorrow. In the name of the Father, and the Son, and the Holy Ghost, amen."

HOURS LATER—after the last of their friends and family had left the house, after all the food had been wrapped and put in the refrigerator—Eve joined her sister and Steven in the living room.

The two were seated close together on the couch, gazing at the fire blazing in the giant hearth. Eve sank down on the end cushion. She leaned forward toward the coffee table in front of her, and moved the humidor holding her father's pipe tobacco away from the edge.

"Lord, I'm tired," she said, kicking off her shoes and tucking her feet under her body.

"Why don't you get some sleep," Steven advised, turning and leaning behind Janet's slight form to look at Eve. "Janet and I can load the dishwasher and clean up the rest of the mess in here."

"Would you?" Eve said, grateful for the offer. The past four days had been nonstop hell for her. Imagine, her parents dying on Christmas Eve. They had been flying back from a working vacation in Mexico to spend the holidays with Eve and Steven.

A thick fog had suddenly enveloped the coastline, and somehow, although he had been flying for more than thirty years, her father had become disoriented and the plane had crashed in the hills a few miles past the airport.

Eve had rushed back from Berkeley, where she had been visiting Steven. Where she had made love with him for the first time. She spent the next three days trying to take care of all the legalities and arrangements for the funeral.

Steven had been wonderful. His strength supported her throughout the ordeal. But now she had reached the end of her tether and she no longer could resist the temporary oblivion that sleep offered.

"I'll see you both in the morning," Eve said, pushing to her feet and slipping them back into her pumps. "I've put fresh sheets on your bed, Janet, and towels in the upstairs bathroom."

"Thanks, Evey."

Eve smiled at Janet's usage of that old nickname.

"Why don't you turn off the phone in your bedroom," Janet suggested. "I'll take any calls so you can sleep in tomorrow as late as you want."

"Thank you, that sounds wonderful," Eve said, slowly crossing the room. Passing the alcove with her piano and the Christmas tree, she paused. The lights hadn't been turned on since her parents' death. She'd put away the ornaments tomorrow, she decided, and have Steven take down the tree. Suddenly feeling vulnerable, she went back to the couch to kiss him and take comfort from a good-night hug.

"Sweet dreams, darling," she said, bending down. But her lips only grazed his mouth and landed on his cheek when he moved his head unexpectedly.

Feeling a bit clumsy, Eve didn't try to embrace him. Instead, she turned to Janet and managed to successfully deliver the kiss she aimed at her sister's forehead.

"Don't you stay up late, either, sweetie. You'll have to tell us the latest about Paris and school tomorrow morning," Eve said, stifling a huge yawn.

Once in her room, she quickly stripped, and then fell into her narrow bed. Feeling very cold, she pulled the covers more tightly around her shaking body. Steven was sleeping in the first-floor guest room just next door. And although they used the same connecting bathroom, it hadn't seemed right for them to share her bed here, under these circumstances. Willing herself to shut off her mind, Eve fell into a deep, dreamless sleep.

SOMETHING, a flush of water and then a loud thump overhead, woke Eve up at five-thirty the next morning.

Thinking Janet might have stumbled over unfamiliar furniture in the dark, Eve quickly threw on her robe and dashed up the staircase to the upper floor.

The door to Janet's studio was half open. Hearing a muffled groan, Eve rushed in, flicking on the light switch to the right of the entryway.

Quickly scanning the room, Eve realized she shouldn't have worried. Janet had not tripped over a chair. She had not fallen out of bed. In fact, she was still in it—safe and sound—lying next to Steven on the pretty, pink-flowered sheets Eve had put on yesterday.

Eve didn't remember how she got down the stairs. The next thing she knew, she was in the bathroom, with waves of nausea overwhelming her as she splashed cold water onto her tearstained face.

An age later, after she had taken a shower, scrubbing her skin raw, Eve dressed in jeans and a sweatshirt, and went out to the living room.

The remains of yesterday's gathering still littered the area. Resolutely making her mind a blank, Eve thoroughly cleaned the downstairs. She was unloading the dishwasher an hour later when Janet walked in, stopping at the doorway.

She was dressed in a blue cashmere sweater and matching slacks. In her black leather flats, she looked tiny and fragile.

"Steve's in the car. We're going back to his place in Berkeley," she began without preamble. "He wanted to talk to you, but I said it would be better for me to explain."

Though waves of pain were washing over her, Eve was silent. She just started putting dishes away in their proper locations in the cabinets to keep from breaking down and sobbing in front of Janet.

"Look, Eve, this wasn't planned," Janet said, taking a step toward her sister. "I guess it was love at first sight for both of us."

"Love? Falling into bed with your sister's fiancé twelve hours after meeting him—half a day after your parents have been put in the ground—is love?" Eve found herself whispering, her voice vibrating with the pain she felt.

"Yes, it is. Why else would I have done such a thing? Whatever you think of me, I am not a monster!" Janet protested.

"And it was love at first sight for him, too?" Eve muttered. "Well, I should have listened to my roommates."

"Roommates?" Janet whispered, her eyes large with obvious confusion at Eve's unexpected reaction.

"It was six months ago, a few days before I graduated...just before Steven and I got engaged. Both of them warned me about him, but I didn't believe them." Eve giggled, knowing she was on the fine edge of hysteria.

"Warned you, about Steve?"

"Yes, Steven...your wonderful Steve. They said while we were dating, he had put the make on them. Both of them, at different times, of course. And of course, that was before he gave me the ring."

Suddenly looking at her hand, Eve wrenched the diamond off her finger and threw it at Janet. "Take this. It's only six months old...should have a lot of mileage left on it. It'll probably last through three or four more fiancées, you can tell Steven.''

Placing the ring in a pocket, Janet took a ragged breath.

''Evey, I know you're hurt, but it's really for the best. Eve? God, I guess there's nothing more to say.'' She turned to leave. ''I'll come down again after the wills are probated and ready to be read.''

''Oh, I don't doubt that for a moment.''

''What are you saying?'' Janet whirled back to face Eve. ''Do you mean I should renounce my inheritance? That I don't have any rights to part of my parents' estate? Well, I didn't get their love, so I'm sure as hell entitled to get something from them, even if it's only money.''

''Not get their love? Are you crazy? After all they did for you, how can you say they didn't love you?'' Eve protested.

''Oh, yes, I forgot. All those tests they put me through. All those special tutors they saddled me with. That wasn't love, it was pity. How could they not pity me, when they had to compare me to you every day.

''Fat, dumb little me...and beautiful, brilliant you. You heard Father Moreno in church yesterday? Straight-A student, captain of the cheerleading squad, class valedictorian. Oh, it was so much fun following behind you all through school. I could see the amazement in the teachers' eyes. 'How can this short, dumpy retard—who can't even read very well—be the wonderful Eve Gray's sister? She *must* have been adopted.' ''

''But, Janet, you're dyslexic...not dumb,'' Eve broke into her sister's tirade. She well remembered all the hours she had spent drilling Janet in her early teen years, when the problem had finally been diagnosed. "And I know Mom and Dad were very proud of your artistic abilities. So was I—"

"Yes, there always was that. Being able to draw was the only thing that kept me from killing myself."

"Janet! Janet, why didn't you ever tell me that you felt like this?" Eve found herself walking toward her sister.

"What, and ruin even one day of your charmed life? Nobody would ever do that to the 'princess,'" Janet scoffed. "But now I'm the thin one...the beautiful one. Steve told me so. And do you know what he called you? An Amazon. You're a big, fat Amazon! So maybe now you'll finally understand how the other half lives."

I GUESS I really do understand now, Eve thought, getting up from the studio floor and once more looking around Janet's empty room. Two days after that confrontation last year, movers had arrived and stripped the house of everything her sister owned.

Steven had called and tried to speak to Eve a few times. But she had been unable to bear listening to his voice. Somehow, all she could hear was him saying the word "Amazon" over and over again. Eve had hung up on each occasion.

Finally, he sent a long, apologetic letter that she forced herself to read.

In it he echoed Janet's excuse about them falling in love with each other at first sight. He wished Eve well, assuring her that all of this was for the best. "You and I were really not suited for each other. We're so much alike, so logical... we would have been bored silly after a few years."

Eve had actually laughed at that last bit of reasoning. Tearing up the pages, she threw the paper in the garbage, mentally consigning Steven to the trash bin, as well.

A month later, at the reading of her parents' wills, Janet and Steven had sat in the lawyer's office, holding hands. Each wore a brand-new wedding band. The diamond engagement ring was noticeably absent from Janet's finger.

Steven, having newly passed the bar, handled Janet's interests . . . very ably, too. Not satisfied that her parents' wills were equitable—with stocks and bonds going to Janet, the house to Eve—he had suggested it would be fairer if all assets were liquidated and the proceeds divided in two. It was in Eve's best interest to do so, he assured her.

And on paper, that might even have been true. But Eve had adamantly refused. As far as she was concerned, it was just a mean-spirited ploy on Janet's part to rob Eve of the only thing she had left to love in this world . . . the house she had grown up in.

So, despite the Christmas card begging for her forgiveness, she was not ready to grant them that absolution. Eve was glad Janet and Steven had not actually been here today. A visit from them would have been one thing too much, after all that had happened to her today . . . No, the past *few* days.

Because while she had been thinking about Janet and Steven, it seemed that her subconscious had been working. And Eve now had the answer to one of her most puzzling questions—how the house had gotten decorated for the holidays.

She had done it, herself, sometime during the last few days. The days she had lost to amnesia.

Lord, amnesia! Eve had once heard a phrase that summarized her life this past year: bad things happen to good people. At least, she had always thought of herself as a good person. And she had no doubts that some pretty rotten things had happened to her in the past twelve months. Death. Betrayal. And now, short-term amnesia.

Unfortunately, it seemed this new year wasn't going to be so wonderful, either. Today she had whacked into a wall and given herself the next closest thing to a concussion—complete with the memory of a nonexistent earthquake.

And since coming back to consciousness in Sam's arms this afternoon, since the devastating kiss in the vestibule downstairs half an hour ago, Eve had found out that infatuation no longer described her feelings for him. It was beyond that. She had gone and fallen in love with a married man.

Even worse, she had somehow let Sam know how she felt. And, evidently due to the sad circumstances in his own life—his wife's condition and her continuing physical problems—Sam had just indicated by his passionate embrace, that he would like Eve to begin an affair with him.

Groaning from the sudden throbbing of her head, Eve concluded it was past time to take some more aspirin. Carefully closing the door to the studio, she went downstairs, got a couple tablets from her bathroom, and decided to down them with a glass of milk.

The kitchen still smelled of rich coffee and somehow vibrated with the lingering aura of Sam Davidson's presence. Not trusting her shaking hands, Eve took the carton and glass to the table and sat in a chair before pouring the milk. After swallowing the pills, she absently picked up the newspaper Sam had put on the table.

It's strange that I've waited this long to find out exactly how many days I've lost, she thought.

It was perhaps a commentary on how confused and upset she had been in the last several hours since hitting her head. Or, more likely, how distracted being in Sam's company had made her.

Eve flipped open the paper to the front page and scanned the masthead for the date.

"No! Absolutely not!"

The pages she balled up flew across the room toward the refrigerator. Bolting from her chair before the paper had even hit the slate floor, Eve ran from the kitchen.

In the living room, she switched on the television and stabbed the channel selector repeatedly until it reached the twenty-four-hour news station.

As the picture sharpened, Eve's eyes focused on the time and temperature statistics that ran along the bottom of the screen.

10:15:10 PM PST *** 60°F *** 16°C *** Wednesday, December 29 *** 10:15:20 PM PST *** 60°F *** 16°C *** Wednesday, December 29 ***

Eve sank to the rag rug in front of the set, watching the numbers parade by for several minutes, trying to figure out what was going on. Something *had* to be wrong... with both the newspaper and this channel.

Otherwise, it meant that she had not lost *any* days to amnesia. Instead, somehow—some way—she had been transported back in time... almost three days.

She was still staring blindly at the set when the phone rang ten minutes later. After hesitating a second, Eve reached for the extension on the nearby end table.

"Eve, it's Sam. Eve, are you there?"

"Yes . . . yes, Sam. What do you want?"

"Now there's a subject I'd better not get into on the phone," he said with a deep, infectious chuckle. "Let's just say, as promised, I'm checking to see that you're doing all right. You are, aren't you?"

"That's debatable," Eve muttered, watching the data flowing across the bottom of her television screen.

"Eve, you sound . . . strange. Maybe I should come back over there."

"No, don't do that! I mean, it isn't necessary."

"All right. Then I'd like you to answer a couple of questions for me."

"Look, Sam, it's late. I'm tired . . ."

"I know. Just humor me. What time is it?"

Eve giggled. She couldn't help it. That was an easy one! "Ten twenty-five and forty-three seconds, p.m., Pacific standard time."

"Ah . . . yes. Guess you're close enough," Sam said dryly, that crooked grin obvious in his voice. "Just one more question and I'll let you go. What's the date?"

Now did she really want to answer that one? Yes. Eve had to know just how messed up she really was.

"Wednesday, December 29," she intoned.

"Got it right in one. Sounds like your mind is as clear as a bell. See you in the morning, love."

"Don't you dare call me that, you lecherous son of a—"

Eve could have gone on, but with a chuckle and the sound of a smacking kiss, Sam had already hung up on her.

"I'm going to tell your wife on you!" she finally yelled at the phone, all the while knowing she could never hurt Amber in that way.

No, but what she *would* do, first thing in the morning, was check with Julie about job opportunities for statisticians in some other facility. Some other city. Some other planet.

Eve slowly got up and dragged herself into the bedroom. A few minutes later she was in bed, the quilt pulled up to her nose. Closing her eyes, she tried to stop shaking and calm herself enough to sleep. However, her mind would not cooperate.

It kept sifting through recent events, trying to find some logical explanation for her situation.

The most fantastic possibility, Eve decided, was that, somehow, she really *had* been tossed back in time. If true, it meant that during the earthquake aftershock, some force had sent her three days into the past—well, fifty-six hours, to be precise.

And now she would relive the events of these next days all over again...sort of. But obviously, not exactly, because things had already happened differently today than in her first go-round of December 29.

Eve had read dozens of science fiction stories with this theme, so she was certainly familiar with the details of the travel-back-in-time option. If it were really possible, she was faced with a dilemma.

It would mean a big earthquake would rupture the Hayward Fault the day after tomorrow, at the stroke of midnight. Freeways would fall, buildings would topple, and hundreds, perhaps thousands, of people would be killed or injured.

Those people could include her sister and Steven . . . along with Hertha Jenkins's daughter and her newborn grandchild. Which meant Eve should not be in bed right now, but on the phone, contacting Janet, Hertha . . . and the authorities. She would have to make them believe her fantastic story, and act on it.

But the main problem with this possibility was Eve didn't believe it herself. Fantasy was one thing, fact—science—was another. And Eve had never heard of any actual proof that time travel was possible, or that anyone had ever *really* experienced it.

Well, no, that's not entirely true, Eve suddenly thought, sitting upright against the headboard of her bed. Her photographic memory dredged up the image of an article she had read several years ago, of experiments done with subatomic particles.

In the procedure, tiny bits of matter, called tachyons, were actually detected *before* they had been created in the laboratory. The scientists involved could only explain the results if the tachyons had traveled back in time, a few microseconds into the past.

Eve shook her head. She was not a tachyon, but rather, a complicated construct of trillions of atoms. There was no way she could imagine having traveled, bodily, into the past. Ridiculous!

She slumped back down, punching her pillow and settling once more. She was on the edge of sleep when the second possibility occurred to her. Maybe she had gone, not into the past, but around the bend. Crackers!

Lord knew, she'd had enough stuff happen to her to have earned a nervous breakdown!

Perhaps she should get out the Yellow Pages directory in the morning and look up a friendly neighborhood psychiatrist. Nah, it was the holiday season, and any doctor worth his fee would be on vacation. But— she smiled to herself—if her life continued in this fashion, she'd probably be advised to follow that course of action right after the first of the year.

The only problem was, deep down, she didn't feel crazy.

No, Eve decided, turning on her back and staring up at the exposed ceiling beams, the most likely answer to all of her strange "memories" was the blow to her head she had sustained today.

It must have produced a vivid, but fallacious series of mental experiences that would account for everything that "seemed" to have happened to her: the preparations for the New Year's party; the event itself; her meeting Amber Davidson; the Hayward Fault earthquake and its aftershock, in which she had fallen and hurt her head . . . the first time.

No, that wasn't right. She had only hit her head once. This afternoon. Then the whole series of false events, including the party and the earthquake, must have been created in her mind during the few minutes she had been unconscious.

Okay, that was probably what had happened.

But, why were the false memories so vivid? They were still compellingly real. In fact, Eve had the almost overpowering urge to go out on the widow's walk to warn everybody about the coming disaster.

And then there were all those *other* things that the head-injury hypothesis didn't address. Like the rearrangement of the furniture in the living room, and the appearance of the Christmas tree.

Now that she knew the date, Eve realized *she* could not have redecorated the house during the days she had lost to amnesia. Because she hadn't lost any days! In fact, it seemed as if she had gained them. Two and a half days to live all over again.

Forcing herself out of this crazy time loop, Eve considered the next item on her mental list...the greeting card from Janet and Steven, which she had found on the mantel this evening. She was absolutely certain she had never seen it before tonight.

But the most inconsistent thing of all had to be Sam Davidson. Why had he changed so dramatically? Until he held her in his arms today in the facility corridor, he had never shown any lustful interest in her. They had been friends, no more. But now...

In self-protection, her mind skittered away from thoughts of just how unlike a friend Sam had been today. Particularly, of how his huge, hard body had felt pressed intimately against hers in the vestibule.

Instead, her overactive brain suddenly offered another explanation for her confusion. The one possibility she had overlooked up to now.

Maybe all of this was just a bad dream.

A long, incredibly detailed nightmare! That would explain everything, including the crazy inconsistencies. So, to get back to normal, all she had to do was wake up. Actually, what she really had to do was fall asleep first...so that she could *then* wake up.

Congratulating herself for being so logical, Eve closed her eyes. After struggling for a long time to clear her mind, she finally drifted off.

Chapter Six

Sam was just getting out of the shower when he heard Eve's voice talking to his answering machine. Wrapping the towel more tightly around his waist, he dashed into the living room and grabbed the receiver. But she had already hung up.

He quickly dialed her number. After four rings *her* answering machine kicked in.

Swearing under his breath at the wonders of modern technology, Sam slammed down the receiver without leaving a message. He then jabbed the replay button on his own device to hear what she had said.

He stood looking at Amber's photograph on the table until the tape rewound and Eve's words once again filled the small room.

"Sam, this is Eve. I thought I was calling early enough to catch you before you left. Maybe you're in the shower, or out for a jog. I guess I should leave a note on my front door in case you've already gone. I mean... Shoot, I sound like a ding-a-ling.

"Anyway, Sam, if you listen to this before you go to work, I just wanted to tell you not to pick me up this morning. A taxi will be here in a minute or two. Say hello to... No, she hasn't met me yet, has she? I

mean...Lord, I'm so confused. Hope I didn't wake...
Oh, oh . . . taxi's here. Got to go. Goodbye."

"Ding-a-ling? I'll give you that, Eve Gray. You
should have added incomprehensible, and just plain
stubborn!" he snarled at the message machine.

Sam then stomped into the bedroom to dress.

"DAMN STUBBORN WOMAN!" Sam muttered for the
umpteenth time as he walked through the building
entrance. Well, he was sick of it. He was going to
march into Eve's office and get her to listen to what he
had to say, even if he had to tie her to the chair to do
it.

Sam was tired of her evasions, tired of trying to
scale the barriers she placed between them . . . tired of
being a "friend" to her. He would make her admit to
the electrifying attraction that charged the very air
whenever they were together. And before this day was
over, their relationship was going to be much
clearer . . . and much, much closer.

"Sam! Glad you're early. Have we got a problem."
Swinging around in the direction of the masculine
voice, Sam was almost barreled over by Jim Creecy,
his deputy security officer.

"What's going on, Jim?"

"Tawny down in cryptography just decoded an
E-mail message from some eco-terrorist organization
threatening to sabotage our data base."

The hefty man grabbed Sam's elbow and steered
him in the direction of the decoding room. After running his ID card through the mechanism at the door,
Sam punched in the proper code for the week. The
lock clicked open, allowing them entrance.

"Tawny, Sam just got in. Show him the message you decoded."

The statuesque young woman got up from her work station, and brought Sam the printout. "I have the early shift this week and found the coded threat while downloading the general notice E-mail, Sam."

Tawny leaned forward. Two of her most obvious attributes invaded his "personal space" as she began explaining her findings.

The provocative little gesture was typical of her flirtatious persona. Sam didn't take it seriously, and just moved back a few inches. His interest lay in another direction... with an obstinate, green-eyed lady, whom he was going to waylay just as soon as he took care of this crisis.

"You can see the iterations of decrypting I did before getting the plaintext," Tawny was saying. "The ciphertext code is really elaborate... with three levels of encryption."

Sam read the final message Tawny had deciphered.

Stop the slaughter. Killing a Tree may be dangerous to your data's health. If the Trees go, so will
the code. Stop the slaughter... save your data
base.

      The Green Gorillas, Friends of the Forest

"Green *Gorillas?*" Sam laughed. "At least this group's got a good sense of humor. Tawny, if this was such a complicated encryption, how did you crack it so quickly?"

"Well, something about it reminded me of a classic case we had in code school. So I surfed the Internet and found what I was looking for there. I discovered that the text had been converted into numbers, and then each digit was raised to an exponent. After that, a modulus was subtracted from the original number, until the result was smaller than the modulus.''

"And that told you what?'' Sam asked, his encryption skills not quite up to Tawny's.

"That the interloper used textbook methods—literally. So even though it's very complex, since I had found the public key on the Internet—that is, the published exponent and modulus—it was a cinch to break.''

"Right . . . if you say so,'' Sam said with a chuckle. "Very well done, Tawny. You really know your stuff.''

"Thanks . . . thank you, Sam,'' she said hesitantly.

Sam was surprised to see a flush rise up Tawny's neck at his compliment. But when he thought about it for a second, he remembered how young she was, and how beautiful.

"Beautiful people'' of both sexes, Sam mused, lived under a double-edged sword at work. They were often hired over their plainer counterparts. But then, their employers tended to see them only as decoration, not taking anything they did seriously.

But putting Tawny's possible problems aside for the time being, Sam sat down at a terminal and switched his mind into hacker mode.

"Let me get on line and do a little tracking to see if our Green Gorillas have left any green footprints.''

Initiating the security batch files he had scripted in the first week after his arrival, Sam began typing. "Look for *CLOAK* . . .''

AN HOUR EARLIER that morning, a cab had let Eve off at the gate of the office complex. She paid the driver and took a furtive look around. Seeing that the coast was clear, she scurried through the parking lot, hoping that she could get inside the building before Sam showed up. She didn't know if she had the moral strength to refuse him if he came on to her again.

"Eve! Yo, wait for me."

Eve automatically cringed, even though she immediately recognized Julie Rosen's voice, not Sam's, calling to her. Julie waved from the next aisle over, where she was locking up her car.

"I heard you fell and bumped your head yesterday," the redhead said when she reached Eve. "I was going to phone last night, but Bob said you needed rest more than a call from me. Are you all right?"

"Oh, I'm fine . . . only a little confused about a few things," Eve answered, touching her temple just below the healing cut.

Confused? What an understatement! She had woken up at six, and immediately jumped out of bed to retrieve the morning paper. Unfolding the pages, Eve had groaned out loud when the masthead informed her that today was December 30th.

So much for the hope she would wake up finding herself back to normal, with the whole experience only an exceptionally vivid extended nightmare.

And now, walking alongside her friend, Eve debated whether or not to tell Julie about the false memories her injury had caused. Maybe talking through the experience with her levelheaded pal would put to rest the almost overwhelming urge Eve had to call the authorities and warn them that maybe—possibly—a big earthquake would hit the Hayward Fault tomorrow night.

But Julie continued talking, even as Eve searched her mind for a way to begin.

"And I also heard Sam Davidson scooped you off the floor into his marvelously muscled, manly arms and carried you over to the clinic."

Eve nodded, trying not to giggle at the mental picture she had just envisioned. In it, scores of people stood gawking while Sam staggered down the corridor, burdened with her not insignificant mass. At least no one saw the kiss he had given her, or she'd never hear the end of it from Julie.

"Well, did this dashing rescue change your mind about Sam?"

"Change my mind?"

"About responding to his interest in you?"

They had gone into the building and reached Julie's office. The redhead stood with one hand on the doorknob.

"Julie!" Eve gasped. "Has it really been that obvious before yesterday?"

"Well, yes, I'd say so. He certainly pumped me enough for information on you. But when Tawny told us about San Diego, I can understand your reluctance. I mean, after Steven, who wouldn't be wary? But even with Sam's reputation, I'm not so sure I'd be able to resist him if I were in your shoes."

"Reputation?" As a devoted husband to his disabled wife? At least, that's what everybody around here thought of him. So had Eve...until yesterday. She was having a hard time following Julie's logic. "Julie, I can't believe you would sanction infidelity. What about Bob?"

"Oh, I meant if I were free, of course." She grinned.

"But...but there's also Sam's wife. We can't forget Amber, Julie!" Although Sam had, last night. And so had Eve, during that impossibly erotic kiss. Lord, she felt so ashamed of herself.

"No, not forget her, but we can't live in the past, Eve. You know that. And about San Diego...well, let's just say it's man's nature to flit from flower to flower. At least, until he meets his Venus's-flytrap!" Julie laughed, and waved goodbye before popping into her office.

Strange. What a really strange conversation, Eve thought, entering her own office. But she was afraid things were likely to get even weirder today, especially when she saw what awaited her on the desk.

At first it seemed like any other memo she had received from her supervisor, John Terrent. The message reminded Eve she was supposed to check the analysis report of the data compiled since December 20th for typos and calculation errors.

The note also instructed her to print out five copies and bring them to this afternoon's meeting of the data rectification committee.

A straightforward and relatively easy assignment, Eve thought. Except for the fact that she remembered having already edited this same data, and had sat through the meeting a day or so ago!

No, that wasn't right. In her memory, the conference had taken place on December 30th. Which was...today.

Sinking down in her chair, Eve pressed trembling fingers to her lips, trying to hold back the scream that wanted to break free. There had to be some mistake. Her memory had always been a faithful ally she could count on. Why had it suddenly turned traitor?

Eve shook her head and straightened her shoulders. *No. I absolutely refuse to crack up,* she stubbornly decided. Her false memories only went up to midnight tomorrow. Surely all she had to do was live through these next two days and everything would be all right again.

Sending up a prayer that she was correct, she reached over to turn on her computer. If getting back to normal meant she had to re-edit the report, and go to a meeting she had already attended, that's exactly what she would do.

Just before noon, she finished the corrections— again. Eve was about to hit the print option when something occurred to her.

If the meeting went according to her recollections of the event, this afternoon her department head would point out an embarrassing compilation error she had made on the bottom of page twelve.

Quickly scrolling down to the area, Eve found she had somehow transposed the same two numbers again. Swearing under her breath, she corrected the mistake with a few defiant keystrokes, and then printed up the five copies her supervisor wanted.

John Terrent wasn't going to have the chance to gloat this time! This time, the report would be perfect.

This time?

AS NATIONAL EMERGENCIES go, fixing this one has been a piece of cake, Sam thought, walking through the hallways toward Eve's office. It had only taken him a couple of hours to find the chief Green Gorilla, a twelve-year-old computer hacker, who was terrific at cracking security codes, but didn't know how to spell the word "guerrilla!"

When Sam had "sniffed" the Gorilla's scent, it led to the facility network account of one of the unit's most trusted employees. The mischievous hacker, who used this access code to gain entrance into the system, had turned out to be the dedicated man's daughter.

Too dedicated for his child, it seemed. The fellow was a single parent, and his daughter, feeling neglected by the long hours he had been putting in recently, had done something designed to really get his full attention.

Sam had just spent the past hour talking to the two. Satisfied no malicious intent had been involved, he decided not to turn the matter over to the authorities. Instead, he had given the young girl a crash course on the consequences of using her computer for practical jokes.

Next time, he had warned, he would bring her up on charges.

Sam had also decided that when Hertha Jenkins came back from her trip to San Francisco, he would ask her to help him turn the young lady away from the "Dark Side" of computer hacking. The little girl had shown an awful lot of programming talent.

One good thing about the interruption, Sam thought, was that it had given him time for his temper to cool down. *Eve can't help but be enchanted by my wonderfully charming self.*

He was grinning when he reached her door and knocked. Not waiting for an invitation to enter, he charged inside.

"Eve, it's lunchtime, darlin'. Don't even think about arguing this time. Let's have some food and a good, long talk..."

Sam stopped halfway into the room when Eve looked up from her computer terminal at the sound of his voice. She was so pale, her eyes looked like huge, green beacons in her face.

"Eve, what's the matter? Is your head bothering you? Do you want to go back to the infirmary?"

"No, there's absolutely nothing wrong with my head!" she protested vehemently, even while rubbing her temple. "I was just doing this report. Again. And I found the error I missed in it the first time. You see, someone else spotted it the last time. I mean... Oh, Sam, I thought I could handle this. I only have to relive the next thirty-six hours, but I'm getting so mixed up."

Eve stood abruptly and then swayed. Before she could fall, Sam had vaulted over the desk and put his arms around her shoulders.

"Whoa, there. Sit down, sweetheart." Lowering her back into the chair, he hunkered down, then cupped her chin to get a good look at her eyes. They appeared clear and normal, but he was still concerned. "You were babbling, Eve. I'm calling Dennis to come look at you..." He reached for the phone.

"No, don't do that!" Eve pushed his hand away from the receiver, knocking over a nearby picture frame in the process. "I'm all right now, Sam. Really, I am. I just didn't have any breakfast."

Sitting upright in her chair, she took a deep breath, and looked at him for a long minute. Then, as if she had made her mind up about something earth-shattering, Eve squared her shoulders.

"Sam, I have to talk to somebody—someone who has an open mind. Someone who reads science fiction! Because something...strange has happened to me. You mentioned lunch. Okay. But I'd rather not go to the cafeteria. It's too...noisy. How about somewhere outside the complex?"

Despite her manner and her words—so serious and precisely logical—Sam felt his mouth lift into a wide smile. Eve needed help, and she had turned to him for it! His day had taken a definite turn for the better. "Sure, darlin', anywhere you want."

"I don't care where it is, but I do have a condition." Eve waited for his nod, indicating that he was listening, before she went on. "I want your solemn promise...I need a sacred oath that if we have lunch together, you won't use any endearments, or try to...touch me...or anything else. Otherwise, I can't go with you."

Sam was about to make a flippant remark. But then he saw the worry, the haunted look of helplessness on Eve's face. He felt shaken to the core, as every protective instinct in his body suddenly shifted into high gear.

"I give you my word, Eve...I won't take advantage of being alone with you during lunch. I'll just listen to your problem, and try to give you whatever advice I can...as your friend."

"Thank you, Sam. I really do need a friend right now." Eve lifted her hand, and Sam held his breath as her fingers came to within a scant inch of his cheek. But then they began to tremble. Abruptly turning away, she bent to retrieve her purse from the bottom desk drawer, and Sam heard the sound of a ragged sigh escape her long, elegant throat.

Trying to recover his own equilibrium, Sam righted the metal frame Eve had knocked over. Expecting a family photograph, he was surprised to see under the glass a long list of something entitled "The Rules." Intrigued, he read the first couple out loud.

"'Rule Number One, The Female Always Makes The Rules. Number Two, The Rules Are Subject To Change By The Female At Any Time, Without Prior Notification To The Male...'"

"Uh-uh, give me that." Eve eased the frame from his hands and turned it facedown on the desk. "Rule Number Three says, 'No Male Can Be Allowed To Know All The Rules.' You shouldn't be reading supersecret stuff like this, Sam," she chided, laughter hidden in the reprimand.

"Well, sor-ry! I had no idea," he apologized. "Supersecret, huh? What organization devised these rules...The Monterey Yentas?"

"I can not divulge the source of 'The Rules,'" Eve deadpanned, rising to her feet. This time she didn't keel over when she got up from the chair. "I'm really starving. Let's go, Sam."

At his car in the parking lot, Sam rolled down both front windows. Feeling a vivid sense of déjà vu, he remembered yesterday's events as he started the engine.

The carefree mood generated by their sparring over "The Rules" seemed to evaporate quickly. They drove in silence along busy Lighthouse Avenue, past dozens of restaurants and shops catering to the horde of visitors Monterey attracted every year.

Just after passing the historic Cannery Row buildings and the world-acclaimed Aquarium, Sam cut over to Ocean View Boulevard. He hadn't been to either attraction yet. It wasn't much fun going alone, without someone to share in the appreciation of a new discovery.

Amber had loved to explore, to search out hidden treasures. But, because he'd made the wrong choice, her carefree companionship had ended three years ago. He had wanted to ask Eve to go with him, but with her attitude...

Sam shook his head in frustration. After a quick glance at her sitting so silently beside him, he checked the still unfamiliar street for his bearings.

The south side of Ocean View was jammed tight with block after block of private residences and houses that had been converted into bed-and-breakfast inns. Many of them had oversize picture windows and wraparound balconies to take full advantage of the incredible vistas provided by Monterey Bay.

Its bright beaches and rocky outcroppings swept for miles from Pacific Grove toward the northwest, to Santa Cruz on the far northeast tip of the Bay.

Just before 17th Street, Sam pulled into a spot in the small municipal parking lot and switched off the engine.

"Why are we at Lovers' Point?" Eve asked after a few seconds, seeming to notice her surroundings for the first time.

Deciding not to take advantage of *that* opening, Sam just said, "I discovered a little food stand over there in the park serving the best Coney Island-style hot dogs I've eaten since leaving Detroit."

He opened his door. "Come on, Eve. I'll get us a couple of chili dogs and some drinks. Why don't you stake out one of those tables down by the beach?"

EVE SANK onto the wooden picnic bench and looked out over the ocean. Several swimmers were braving the winter water, dressed in wet suits as colorful as the rainbow. Watching their energetic snorkeling among the abundant marine life in the clear waters just emphasized to her how exhausted she felt.

All she wanted to do was go back home and sleep. Probably her brain's way of coping with the overwhelming situation in which she found herself, Eve reasoned.

What had Julie said this morning? "We can't live in the past."

Well, sweetie? a nasty little voice in her head gibed. *Isn't that exactly what you're going to do...live three days of your past life all over again?*

No! She was not doing that, Eve forcefully told the voice. She just *thought* she had lived these days already. Eve rubbed her suddenly cold hands together, feeling as if she were teetering on the edge of an emotional abyss. With her eyes mesmerized by the incoming waves, her mind engaged in yet another round of speculation. Was there any way she could figure out which of her memories was real and which had resulted from her injury? Hopefully, talking to Sam would help.

"Here's your Polish sausage topped with lots of onions and chili. I also got you a diet soda." As if she had conjured him up, Sam stood in front of Eve, holding out a cardboard tray containing the food. "Hope that's all right with you."

He had loosened his tie and undone the top button of his dress shirt. The flaps of his beautifully tailored dark blue wool suit danced in the breeze, calling attention to his trim waist and narrow hips.

But Eve found her attention snared by the vee of brown skin revealed at the opening in his shirt. She wondered if his skin was as smooth and warm as it looked. If his arms could provide the safe haven she desperately needed.

"Is this sausage all right, Eve?" Sam's puzzled voice finally broke her fascination.

"Oh, thanks, it's fine...just how I like it," she mumbled, taking her portion from him. While she chewed the delicious sausage, Eve hoped Sam couldn't see the flush of embarrassment running rampant over her cheeks. She had demanded an oath from him to behave. So why couldn't *she* keep better control of runaway longings?

But Sam must not have noticed. He just sat down on the bench and attacked his own hot dog with strong, white teeth. "So what's the legend?" Sam asked when his food was half gone.

"Legend? What do you mean, legend?" His simple question seemed too much for her to handle at the moment.

"A place called Lovers' Point must have some sort of tragically romantic story attached to it." He indicated the bronze nameplate on the small monument to their right.

"Actually, Sam... Actually..." Eve couldn't stop the laughter that bubbled up. But she tried to clamp down hard on the giggles threatening to escalate into hysteria. "You see, the original name was Lovers' of Jesus Christ Point, because outdoor gospel meetings were once held here."

"Ah, Eve, that's wonderful," he said, joining her infectious merriment.

His deep chuckle was such an attractive sound, Eve stopped laughing and found herself staring at him again.

"What's wrong...got mustard on my nose?" he queried.

"No, I was just thinking of something, nothing important," Eve denied, appalled that no matter how she fought them, her feelings for this man would not die. In fact, if anything, they had deepened since she'd regained consciousness in his arms.

As he had done on a couple of occasions, Sam breached the facade of her words to expose the hidden thoughts that were troubling her mind.

"Eve, we have to talk. About what happened yesterday, and last night. In fact, we have to discuss what's been happening between us since the day we met. You've got to know how I feel about you. And from the way you kissed me yesterday, you must be...attracted to me, too."

"Sam, you promised! You gave me your word!"

Eve was ready to bolt. But Sam's agitation stayed her. He was running his long fingers through his dark hair in obvious frustration.

"But, Eve, as promised, I am not touching you. And I haven't said any sweet words to you. But I want to! Tell me, why won't you give us a chance? Why can't we see if our feelings for each other couldn't develop into a relationship?"

"Relationship? What kind of relationship would that be?" Eve countered, even as a traitorous arrow of joy pierced her heart at his suggestion. The strength of that emotion made her pause, and then acknowledge, "Okay, I'll be truthful. This hasn't been one-sided. I can't deny I feel...something for you, Sam. But it's wrong! How can you even think of asking me to have an affair with you? I could never do that to Amber!''

"Affair! Amber?'' Sam jumped up, standing huge and glowering over her. "What has Amber got to do with this?''

"Sam! How dare you forget about your wife?'' Eve challenged, having to crane her neck to see his angry face.

"Of course, I'll never forget Amber, or what I did to her. I've mourned about her and the accident long and hard. But, Eve... that was more than three years ago I can't live with one foot in the past any longer. In the four weeks since I met you, my growing feelings for you have helped me finally come to terms with reality. And reality is that I'm alive... and Amber is dead.''

Chapter Seven

"Dead! Did you say Amber is dead?" Eve whispered her confusion, but she hadn't misunderstood him. "When, Sam? When did she die?"

"Oh, don't tell me your good friend Julie didn't pass along the fact that I've been a widower for three years," he grated, his face as unforgiving as granite. "I told her that much during one of her little interrogations when I first got to Monterey. But I didn't think she needed to know Amber died in a car crash, on our honeymoon."

It was a good thing Eve was seated, because the world seemed to spin faster and then slower, smearing the landscape before her eyes. Squeezing her lids shut, she tried to assimilate this latest blow to her sense of reality.

"But I met her, Sam," she whispered. "I remember meeting Amber at—"

At the New Year's Eve party that hadn't happened yet? Or had she just seen Amber in a complicated vision induced by the blow to her head? Oh, she didn't know which way was up anymore!

"Eve, how could you have met her?" Sam's voice was rough with anger. "I just told you, because I made a wrong decision on the road, she bled to death the day after our wedding. While all I got was a cut on my lip.''

Sam's deep blue eyes became even darker. His gaze seemed to turn inward. Eve might have thought the rest of him had turned to stone, if a sea breeze hadn't blown a lock of his thick, black hair onto his wide forehead.

But then a shudder racked his broad shoulders, and Sam ripped the tie off his neck. Jamming it into a pocket, he abruptly wheeled around and strode to a stairway leading down to the lip of the sandy beach. Plowing to the water's edge, he turned west, and then continued his march along the wet sand in that direction.

Realizing she still held a half-eaten sausage in her hand, Eve tossed it and the rest of their interrupted meal into a nearby trash container. Hiking the strap of her purse securely onto her shoulder, she firmly put everything else out of her mind for the moment and set out after Sam.

But before she had taken two steps into the bright sand, her shoes sank, impeding her forward motion. With a sigh of exasperation, Eve removed the low heels, stuck them in her suit jacket pockets, and continued on in her stockinged feet.

Eve didn't try to catch up with Sam; it would have been impossible to match his angry strides. But she kept him in sight among the other people strolling by the shore. She hoped the effort it took to slog his way through the sand would drain away his rage at her.

He finally stopped at a rocky outcrop, his large body sagging back against it.

Eve slowly approached him, not knowing if he would welcome her presence or not. Out of breath, she sank down on the noon-warmed sand a few feet away from him.

He stood looking up at the wheeling sea gulls and puffins for endless minutes. Finally, he turned his gaze on her.

"I'm sorry for yelling at you, Eve. I thought I had dealt with the accident and Amber's death long ago. Haven't had a flashback in over a year."

"Oh, Sam. *I'm* so sorry if what I said about your wife made you dredge up all that pain again. But I really didn't know about her death . . . Finding it out is the worst shock in two days filled with them. I mean, I asked you to have lunch today, because I wanted to tell you about the strange things happening to me since yesterday. But now . . ."

But now, what could she possibly say to him after this discovery?

While Eve sifted through the hopeless jumble of her thoughts, Sam came over and sat on the sand beside her. His huge body blocked the constant sea breeze, and when he reached over to pick up her hand, Eve suddenly felt ten degrees warmer.

"Tell me what's been troubling you, sweetheart. Tell me everything," he coaxed, capturing her hand with both of his.

The instant Sam touched her, Eve mentally released him from the vow she had demanded of him in her office. That oath no longer seemed to have any validity. All Eve knew was that the firm contact of his skin on hers somehow made her feel more anchored to the world than she had been in a long time.

Using the strength seeming to flow into her from him, she tried to regroup her mental forces, to use the logic everybody at work always teased her about.

In sorting out her confusing thoughts, one thing was very clear to Eve—after Sam's emotional outburst, she could *not* start her explanation by mentioning Amber again. Even if meeting his wife had been in a... Just what should she call that whole set of false memories? A hallucination? An illusion... a vision? Okay, she'd call it a vision.

So, perhaps it would be best if she began with the Hayward earthquake she seemed to have experienced in her... vision. And then, tell him about the aftershock tossing her into the wall. Okay, that was a good way to start.

"Sam, I guess what I want to tell you is that since yesterday, I've been having visions." Well, that certainly wasn't what she had planned to say, but it was a beginning.

"Visions? From the hit on your head?" Sam's grasp on her hand tightened. "Eve, you should go to the hospital, or at least see your regular doctor right now. He can tell you if you need an X ray or a CAT scan..."

"Well, Dennis didn't seem to think it was necessary, but you're probably right," Eve conceded. Yet she found she *had* to tell Sam about her experiences. She had always kept her feelings to herself, but now she felt the need to open up to him, as she could never do with Steven, or her parents...or *anybody* else in her life. "Sam, before we go, would you just listen to me about these visions?"

A frown deepened the line between Sam's dark eyebrows. Eve could see indecision in his eyes.

"All right, Eve." He finally nodded. "I guess a few minutes won't make much difference."

Taking a deep breath, Eve waded back into the sea of her bewilderment. "Okay, I'll try to give you a bare-bones outline, Sam. I think all of this started when I hit my head yesterday. When I regained consciousness, I had a new set of memories. Memories that made it seem to me that I'd already lived from that point on Wednesday afternoon, up to midnight, Friday... New Year's Eve. Then, during the facility party, something occurs—an earthquake and another fall—which somehow tosses me back into the past, to the afternoon of Wednesday, December 29th."

"Earthquake? Didn't you mention..." Sam stopped and just nodded to Eve to continue.

"Well... anyway, since waking up in the corridor, I've felt like I'm in a time loop and have been reliving the past two and a half days all over again."

"You've been reliving the past?" Sam's voice was almost inaudible. His gaze turned inward again, but only for a second. "Everybody's had that fantasy, Eve. To go back to some event and do things differently... to try to change the past."

"I know that, Sam. But don't you see, I really feel like I'm actually doing it!"

"Whoa, Eve. Sorry, but you've completely lost me. Are you saying you've been involved in some sort of extended déjà vu, since yesterday?"

"No, it's not just déjà vu, because, as I said before, I also seem to know about the future. And I feel like I've already lived it, up to midnight tomorrow, anyway. Sam, listen. I remember helping decorate the cafeteria tomorrow afternoon for New Year's. And then I have memories of actually going to the party, where I meet . . ."

Where Eve had met Amber Davidson.

No, she realized she could *not* have met Sam's wife. And she never would! He just told her Amber had died on their honeymoon, three years ago.

Sam wouldn't lie about such a thing, just to get her into his bed, would he? Of course not! It would be too easy for Eve to check with Julie about his claim.

Julie?

"Oh, my God, I forgot about Julie . . . and Hertha and Tawny!" *This is far worse than I thought!*

"What . . . what is it?" Sam moved closer and put his arm around Eve's shoulders. "Sweetheart, what is wrong?"

"Sam . . . Sam. I just realized there are more than three screwed-up days involved here. My memory of the entire month of December must be false, too. Because, during the last four weeks, almost from the moment I met you, I thought you were married. I mean, I believed Amber was still alive. In fact, in those memories, Julie and Hertha and Tawny—along with everybody else at the facility—thought she was alive, too. We were all excited about meeting her tomorrow night at the New Year's Eve party."

Sam just sat there, looking stunned. Eve felt equally poleaxed. How could she have such a detailed set of recollections that couldn't be right? Was it possible that a bump to the head could conjure up a whole month of false memories, plus a three-dimensional Amber, with her carrot-red hair and wonderful Australian sense of fun? And what about the devastating earthquake? It still seemed horribly real to Eve.

*Dennis was wrong. That blow to my head must have
made scrambled eggs of my brain!*

"That's it! We're going to see your doctor right
now," Sam declared, standing and then carefully easing Eve to her feet.

"Yes. No. Oh, Sam, I can't go see him. At least, not
yet."

"What do you mean, not yet? Eve, head injuries are
nothing to fool around with."

"Sam . . . don't you realize what the worst thing in
my vision of the future is?"

"My God, what more?" Sam muttered, squeezing
his eyes shut for a second.

Eve automatically put her hands on Sam's wide
shoulders, somehow needing their strong support to
deliver her last revelation. In response, he gathered her
close with one hand, while using the other to brush
away a windblown strand of honey-blond hair from
her eyes.

The tender gesture almost derailed her train of
thought, but Eve sternly forced her mind back on
track.

"Sam, you remember the earthquake I just mentioned to you...and to Dennis yesterday?" She waited
for him to nod. "Well, according to my vision, at exactly five after eleven tomorrow night, there will be a
terribly destructive tremor on the Hayward Fault. The
details of that disaster seem absolutely real to me."

Eve tugged on the sleeve of Sam's suit jacket in her
agitation.

"Do you see what my biggest problem is, Sam?
What if my visions are real, the result of some sort of
precognition? What if I have the opportunity to warn
everybody, and I don't take it, just because I think this

is all the product of hitting my head? Sam, what if I do nothing and thousands are injured, or die in the San Francisco area...including my own sister and her husband who live up there?''

"Oh, Eve, sweetheart, I didn't realize how much you've been going through. And I've just been adding to your problems!"

Sam wrapped his arms around Eve's shoulders, pulling her closer. With sudden need, she put her own arms under his suit jacket and around his waist. Eve held on tight to the only solid object in her careening universe.

The soft, tender kiss Sam brushed back and forth upon her lips seemed only meant to reassure her. Eve felt he just wanted to tell her with the salute that she was safe, and everything would be all right.

But even this light touch of his lips provoked a stab of fire in her that made Eve groan with sudden need.

Pulling his head back at the sound of her sensual distress, Sam anxiously examined her face.

"Eve, is it your head again?"

"Not my head, Sam. But I ache everywhere else," she breathed, and then gasped when she realized just what she had revealed.

Taking a step away from him, it was her turn to apprehensively examine his features. She didn't quite know what she expected to see, but it wasn't the amusement spreading across his face.

"You do pick your moments, lady," Sam said, with a rough chuckle, indicating with his chin the dozen people wading in the nearby ocean surf. "And don't think I won't remind you of your little Freudian slip sometime soon. But we really should get your head looked at first, sweetheart."

"I know... I know, Sam. But before we go to the doctor, I have to stop at my house first and find my sister's new phone number. It'll make me feel better if I call her and ask her to come down for a visit tomorrow... just in case. And even without these visions of an earthquake, I've realized that we have to...talk... After all, she's the only family I have left, and no matter what she's..."

Lord, there I go again, wanting to tell Sam every deep, dark secret, Eve thought as she abruptly halted her runaway tongue. It was just that she knew talking to him about Janet and Steven would make her feel so much better... would somehow help heal that still painful wound.

And as if understanding just how important it was for her to contact Janet immediately, Sam nodded his head.

"I guess it's okay to swing by your house. We're less than five minutes from there. All right, let's go, Eve."

He took her elbow, helping her walk back through the sand. At the edge of the stairway he knelt to brush off her narrow feet and slip on the shoes she handed to him.

It was such an intimate yet caring gesture, Eve felt tears prick her eyes. She couldn't remember the last time she had felt someone so concerned about her well-being.

But with a sudden twinge, Eve did recall something else. At the New Year's party of her vision, Sam had treated Amber in just this way.

It was so hard to believe she had been mistaken about those crystal-clear recollections. Yet she must have been. Sam had been a widower for three years.

And that meant he was *not* out of bounds. Sam was free!

The idea was so electrifying, Eve could hardly keep from running to the car. She might not understand the complex hallucinations about the future she had experienced, but she wanted to race toward any fate that might include Sam.

AFTER THEY PULLED UP to Eve's home, Sam didn't have a chance to take off his seat belt before Eve shed hers and was out of the car.

But instead of racing after her, he found himself walking slowly up the redbrick path toward her front door. The strange conversation on the beach played again in his head.

The whole episode was crazy... the result of Eve's head injury, he was sure. And yet, some of what she had said made sense to him.

It was hard to believe Julie had never mentioned Amber's death, but if Eve really had been unaware of it, that would explain why she had rebuffed his every invitation during the last month.

She had thought he was a married man!

Frustrated as he had been by her attitude, he found himself admiring the strength of her character. He had known all along that she had been as strongly attracted to him as he was to her.

Yet she had fought those feelings, absolutely refusing to have anything to do with him...beyond sharing a few coffee breaks in the cafeteria, while a cast of hundreds looked on.

Smiling at the image, Sam went into the house, where Eve stood at the fireplace mantel, reading the inside message of a colorful Christmas card.

"My sister sent me this." She held up the greeting. "There's supposed to be a piece of paper enclosed with an address and phone number. But it's not here. Maybe I put it in the kitchen."

Sam followed her into that room, where she walked over to a combination bookcase and pulldown desk.

"I keep my bills and recent correspondence in here," she said, opening the desk and quickly going through the neatly organized papers and envelopes inside. "Nope, not here, either. Darn! Maybe I just threw it away."

Eve looked over to the trash receptacle standing at the end of the counter. Getting a clean plastic bag from the undersink cabinet, she opened the bucket's hinged lid.

"Good thing garbage day isn't until tomorrow. Come on, Sam...hold this new bag open for me. Hope it's in here, because if not, we'll have to go through the week's worth of garbage stored out behind the garage."

"Oh, joy, what a wonderful way to spend the afternoon," he said, rolling his eyes even as he grabbed the bag.

"Shoot, guess we go out to the garage," Eve pronounced a few minutes later when they struck out with the kitchen trash. She crossed to the door leading to the backyard. "Sam, I was only kidding about you rooting through the old garbage out there. I'll be back in a few minutes."

"What do you mean? I wouldn't miss it for the world."

Sam followed her outside, and then stopped dead. "Wow, Eve this is fantastic. I didn't know your house sat on a park."

He stood just outside the door, one foot on a curving brick path leading into the most inviting woodland scene he had ever seen on private property. Giant stands of eucalyptus flanked the far reaches of the area, but there were also Monterey Pines, cypress, and huge California pepper trees creating scattered oases, under which flowering shrubs and masses of shade-loving perennials bloomed.

"Actually, there are only two acres left of the original tract. What you see on the sides and at the back are wide swaths of eucalyptus that divide all the adjacent properties. My neighbors and I are just caretakers of the eucalyptus, even though they're on our land. You know, because of the butterflies."

"Butterflies?"

"That's right, you're a newcomer. Watch," she said, clapping her hands together three times.

Even before the last sharp retort had rent the quiet garden, a huge, orange-and-black cloud of whispering wings lifted from the eucalyptus groves and scattered into the leaf-filtered sunlight.

"Monarchs. 'Fragile children of the air,' I've heard them called," Eve said, looking at the fluttering insects with her head tilted back. "But these beauties are really very tough. The adults migrate here from as far away as Canada to spend the winter months. I've also read that those living east of the Rockies fly more than two thousand miles into the high mountain forests of Mexico."

The monarchs settled back into the trees, by the dozens. "This place is more than beautiful, Eve." Sam's eyes surveyed the huge yard and the nearby flagstone patio with its wide, comfortable-looking redwood furniture.

"I'd like to show you the rest of the gardens, but the garbage awaits," Eve said with a soft smile when his attention finally returned to her face.

She pivoted and led Sam along another brick path. They went around a detached two-car garage to a hidden utility area. Several large trash buckets stood there on a concrete strip.

"Their names are Janet and Steven Lange, and I guess it will be a Berkeley address we're looking for. I just hope I didn't tear the thing to bits, or burn it in the fireplace," Eve muttered, taking out the first bag.

A question formed on the tip of Sam's tongue about Eve's last statement. But quelling his curiosity, he got to work, finally locating the slip of paper in the second plastic bag of the first bucket.

"Bingo," he said, holding up the food-stained sheet. Handing her the paper, he gave in to his need to know. "Eve, if it's not too nosy, may I ask why you'd throw this away without recording the information?"

"Oh...well, I usually remember addresses and phone numbers... But in this case, I might have tossed the information because my sister and I had a horrible argument last year."

That terse explanation seemed to hang in the air between them during the short walk back to the living room. But once inside, something compelled Eve to go to the fireplace and pick up one of the photographs displayed there. She suddenly realized that she needed Sam to understand about her anger with Janet. If only she could do it without having to relive all the grimy details.

"This is my sister Janet," she began, handing him the frame. "Well, I guess she doesn't look much like this anymore. She's all grown up and married now.

Anyway, last year Janet and Steven did something I felt was unforgivable. And I must not have changed my mind when their card arrived, so I threw away their new address and phone number. At least, that's what I *think* I must have done.

"The thing is, Sam, I don't remember getting the card with its message. That month of false memories I told you about at the beach seems to have overlaid everything that really happened to me in December. Lord, what a mess."

"Especially for someone who's always been able to remember everything." Sam put his arm around her shoulders and held Eve close for a few seconds before releasing her.

"Exactly," she agreed, trying valiantly to remain cool when his very touch had made her heartbeat kick up into overdrive. "But what's amazing, Sam, is even if my vision of a coming earthquake is false, just the possibility of Janet being in danger has made me realize I should try to reestablish some sort of relationship with her."

Because the fact she stole Steven doesn't matter to me anymore. Steven doesn't matter to me anymore! Eve reeled with the sudden understanding that her feelings for her ex-fiancé were nothing when compared to the overwhelming emotions she felt for Sam.

"Yet, you didn't throw away the card." Sam pointed to the beautiful greeting on the mantel.

Trying to keep her voice from revealing how shaken she still was, Eve said lightly, "Oh, she obviously painted it. Maybe I was keeping it as an investment. An original Janet Gray will probably be worth a fortune someday." *No, it's Janet Lange now,* she corrected herself.

"Don't try that Scrooge act on me, Eve. I've heard from quite a few sources what a kind heart you've got." Sam smiled down at her and deposited a light kiss on her nose. "And are these your parents?" He nodded to the portrait photograph her mom and dad had posed for a few months before their deaths.

"Yes." She looked at her parents, and found tears threatening. Her tall, white-haired father; her tiny, dark mother. Their deaths still made no sense to her.

"You resemble your dad," Sam commented. "And your sister takes after your mom. Where do your parents live?"

"This was their home, Sam," Eve said around the lump in her throat. "They died this time last year...in a plane crash."

"Oh, Eve, you've gone through so much. But things are going to be better from now on, for both of us. I swear it."

Sam's lips electrified her mouth, brushing back and forth over supersensitive tissues until Eve vibrated with need.

Wanting nothing more than to drag him to her bed, Eve nonetheless forced herself to pull back.

"Talk about picking your moments, Sam. I've got to make that call to Janet."

He looked like he was going to protest, but instead just nodded to the nearby phone.

With her hands shaking at the thought of talking to her sister, Eve went over to the instrument and punched out the Berkeley number. But there was no answer. And even when their message machine kicked in, the device gave her no opportunity to speak.

"When it goes right to the dial tone after their message, that means the tape is full, doesn't it, Sam?"

"Either that, or the machine's broken," he observed.

Eve looked at her watch; it was almost one. *Not too late...not too late at all,* she thought as a plan formed in her mind.

"Uh...Sam, shouldn't you be going back to work? Lunchtime is almost over."

"I thought we'd agreed I would take you to your doctor's office for a checkup, Eve." His face had turned deadly serious. "What nefarious scheme is brewing behind those innocent green eyes, you little witch?"

"I hate it when you read my thoughts. But according to Rule Number Eight, 'The Female Can Change Her Mind At Any Point In Time.' And of course, Number Nine is 'The Male Must Never Change His Mind Without The Written Permission Of The Female.'"

Her quip hadn't taken the scowl off his face, as she had intended. Sam just continued to stare at her as if she were a naughty child.

"Sam...look, I'm sorry, but I just can't leave this without making more of an effort to contact my sister. I have got to go up there. At the most, it's a three-hour drive to Berkeley. I'd never forgive myself if something really did happen and I didn't warn them."

"Eve—" he began ominously.

"Sam, I promise I'll see my doctor in the morning, even though I'm feeling fine. See...my hands are steady. I can touch my nose with a finger when my eyes are closed. I can walk a straight line, too." She demonstrated her claims with a teasing smile.

"All right, all right. I admit that except for your screwed-up memory, you're not exhibiting any other sign of brain damage. But make the appointment for the morning anyway, and I'll drive you."

"Oh, you don't have to drive me to the doctor. He's just up the street."

"No, I meant I'll drive you to Berkeley right now."

"Sam! It's not necessary."

"Eve, no matter what you say about how wonderful you feel, you had a nasty bump on the head yesterday. So, I either drive you to Berkeley or to the doctor. Take your pick."

Chapter Eight

Eve didn't have to mull over the ultimatum for more than a second. Now that she knew he wasn't married, the opportunity to drive all the way up to Berkeley and back with Sam was more than attractive.

"All right, Sam. Thanks for the offer. Just give me a minute to change out of this suit and make a call to Julie. I'll let her know I'm taking the rest of the afternoon off. Do you want to go to your place to change?" She indicated his business attire.

"No, I have a heavy jacket in the car trunk if I need it. I want to get going so we're not driving in the dark," Sam said as Eve walked toward the hallway leading to her bedroom. "Don't forget you're also going to make an appointment with your doctor, okay?"

"Okay, Daddy," she demurred, but then laughed out loud.

"Brat," he said indulgently to her closing door.

A second later, Eve's head popped out again. "I forgot. You'll probably want to use the facilities to wash up. Go down to the end of the hall and then turn left into the guest bedroom. The bathroom off of it has some new toothbrushes and toothpaste in the medicine chest. Feel free to use one, if you'd like."

"Thanks, I will. No matter how delicious they were, I don't think other people will appreciate the lingering bouquet of chili and onions." He grinned, then, taking off his jacket, folded it over the arm of her father's recliner.

Feasting her eyes on Sam's fullback shoulders—and his perfect tight end—Eve watched him stride down the hallway. She couldn't move until the gorgeous man disappeared into the correct door.

Dancing back into her own room, Eve suddenly felt like a teenager who had just been asked out by the football team's star player.

With difficulty, she resisted getting up on the bed and bouncing for joy, as she might have done at fifteen. Instead, she stripped out of her suit and quickly washed up in the bathroom. After brushing her teeth, she tied her hair into a ponytail with a rose-colored scarf.

As she arranged her hair, Eve made a quick check of the cut on her head. The butterflies were holding and the scalp surrounding the area looked good. No redness, no other signs of infection. She also realized her head no longer hurt. Gone were yesterday's stabbing pains. She just prayed her memory would make a similar quick recovery.

Back in the bedroom, Eve put on a pair of dark gray wool slacks, a pink, long-sleeved silk blouse, and a heavy black, cable-knit sweater.

Slipping on her moccasin loafers, she sat on the bed. Using the phone extension, Eve made a late-morning appointment for the next day with her doctor. Her second call was to Julie Rosen.

"Hi, Julie, this is Eve."

"Eve! I didn't see you at lunch. What's up, kid?"

"Julie, I'm at home . . . and I won't be coming back to work this afternoon. I've also made an appointment to see my doctor tomorrow morning. Would you please tell my department head the reports for this afternoon's meeting are on my desk?"

"Sure, sweetie, I'll tell John. Still feeling the after-effects of the accident?"

"Sort of," Eve said, not really lying. "Julie, there's something I have to ask you. Something we discussed this morning. Sam's wife . . . Amber. I was talking to . . . someone about her death . . ."

"Oh? Did you find out something more about how she died, Eve?"

So it was true. Sam really was a widower.

"Uh . . . no. Not really, just confirmation that it happened three years ago," Eve answered belatedly. She really didn't want to reveal the other things Sam had told her. He was still so broken up about his role in his wife's death, Eve could understand why he didn't want the details to become public knowledge.

"Well, as I said before, Amber must have been very young when she died. But I guess we'll never know. Sam is so close-mouthed about everything. Must have been a clam in his last incarnation."

Eve held the phone away from her ear and stared at it. She was sure Julie had said something just like that when they were decorating the cafeteria, in her vision of December 31st.

"Eve? Are you still there?" her friend's voice called thinly from the receiver.

"Sorry, I'm here. Julie, do you mean you really don't know anything else about Amber Davidson?"

"Not a thing. Sam still pumps me about you, though. Don't worry, I don't tell him anything that might embarrass you...like what a good kid you are."

"Gee, thanks, I think. But didn't he say what nationality Amber was?" Eve persisted.

"Nationality? Wasn't she American?"

"I'm...not sure. Uh, Julie, one more thing. Tawny found out something about him in San Diego. Could you refresh my memory?"

"Since when does that memory of yours need refreshing, sweetie?"

"Humor me, Julie? Just pretend I never heard anything about it."

"Okay, okay. Tawny has a friend, Victoria, who works at the naval base on North Island. Victoria told her all about Sam's year down there. Quite a Casanova, it seems."

Eve's hands suddenly went cold and she felt a painful lurch in her chest. Something that had just begun to flower inside her heart withered as though it had been struck by a killing frost.

"As I said this morning," Julie went on, "he flitted from flower to flower. According to Tawny's friend, Sam dated and bedded half of the available females at the naval station."

"I'm well aware of all this flower-flitting stuff he did, of course," Eve said carefully.

"Of course. But I'm sorry that you are, because Sam's a great guy. And maybe he's turned over a new leaf...to continue with my botanical metaphor. As far as I know, he hasn't gone out with anyone since he's been here. So, I still think you should say yes the next time he asks you for a date. Although it would probably give the poor fellow a heart attack if you ac-

cepted. Especially since he's all but begged you to go
out with him every day for the past four weeks."

Eve rubbed her head. Why couldn't she remember
any of this? He had asked her out each day since they
met . . . and she had refused?

Well, at least she could understand why she hadn't
wanted to have anything to do with Sam Davidson in
the past month. Even though it seemed he really was
a widower, Eve wouldn't have gone out with a Don
Juan. She wasn't interested in a man who couldn't
keep his pants zipped around a female . . . any female.
In that, he appeared to be just like Steven!

"Well, thanks for the information, Julie," she finally said. *And thanks for keeping me from making
another terrible mistake.* "See you tomorrow afternoon."

"Right. It's a Dress Down Day, isn't it? And the
decorating committee is meeting in the cafeteria at..."

"At one..." Eve supplied from her suspect memories.

"That's right. I just hope Hertha gets back from
San Francisco by then. Haven't heard if it was a boy
or girl," Julie complained with a laugh.

"Oh, I predict that Hertha's new grandchild is a
girl—nine pounds, seven ounces. Melody Anne by
name."

"She called you, Eve!"

"No, just a guess, Julie." Hopefully a wrong one,
Eve told herself. It would mean she was off base about
the earthquake, too.

"Now stop that. It's hard enough liking someone
who's so gorgeous, and talented, and brilliant. If you
start predicting the future, too, you're not going to
have any friends."

Eve hung up the phone, still chuckling. Somehow, Julie always managed to make her laugh.

SAM WATCHED Eve walk back into the living room. The smile lighting her face made her incredibly beautiful. But when she noticed him standing there, the humor drained away, leaving an expression reflecting wariness and withdrawal; something he was all too familiar with from her.

Dammit, he wasn't going to let her put up those barriers again! After the way she had responded to him on the beach, and finally revealed some of her problems to him, he knew Eve was beginning to trust him...and maybe, just maybe, she felt more than that.

Which meant he was going to consolidate the gains he had made today. He was going to stick like glue to Eve. Even if it meant driving her up to Berkeley, on the strength of the cockeyed idea that she needed to personally warn her sister about the possibility of an impending earthquake.

Sam didn't believe in precognition, or whatever had caused Eve to feel like a Big One was due to hit the Hayward Fault tomorrow night. But he knew if he didn't go to Berkeley with her, she would find some way to go without him. And he was not about to let that happen.

Eve was going to be stuck with him for the trip up north, for the journey back...and just maybe for the rest of their lives.

"So, are you ready to go?" he asked blandly, already steeling himself for what he knew would happen next.

"Sam...I've been thinking. Maybe it would be a better idea if you just dropped me at the bus station..." Eve began, right on cue.

"Nope, not a good idea at all." *Boy, this woman is pigheaded!*

"But I don't want to inconvenience you...driving all that way."

"No inconvenience, I love to drive." Now that was a downright lie, but she didn't have to know about him and freeway driving.

"Well..."

"Come on, Eve, we can beat afternoon rush-hour traffic through San Jose and the other cities up north if we get out of here right now."

"Oh, all right. Just let me try my sister's number once more." Eve punched the buttons, but shook her head when the answering machine didn't give her an opportunity to leave a message.

"Maybe they're out of town," she said hopefully. "They may not be back before tomorrow night."

"And then again, maybe they will," Sam said pointedly.

"Right. Well, at least I can leave a note under their door. Okay, let me get some snack food so we can push right on through." She headed toward the kitchen doors.

"Want me to bring along some of your music tapes?" Sam asked.

"Good idea. Mozart...but not the fortieth. And anything else you like."

Sam went to the tape deck and noticed that the forty-second Mozart symphony he had listened to last night was still in the mechanism. After rewinding it, he ejected the cassette to take along, and then picked some other music at random. Why didn't she want Mozart's fortieth? It was one of his favorites.

"All ready," Eve said from the doorway a few minutes later, hefting a brown paper bag.

Without saying a word, Sam took the bag and headed out the front door. Eve found her large leather purse, and after locking up, joined Sam in his car.

"I guess I have enough gas for the trip." Sam pointed to the indicator. "But what about a map?"

"Oh, after four years of driving back and forth at vacations and semester breaks, I could navigate the route between Monterey and Berkeley blindfolded in a fog. Just get over to Del Monte Avenue and take it to Highway 1. That'll merge with 101, and we'll stay on it until San Jose, where we switch to the 880 freeway," Eve suggested.

"Roger on all that . . . I'll rely on your vast experience. So, have you always lived in this area?" Sam asked, pulling away from the curb and popping an Erik Satie recording into his tape player.

"Born and bred on the Monterey Peninsula," she said, letting the deceptively simple piano line of the composer's *Three Gnossiennes* wash over her.

She remembered learning these pieces and loving how Satie had created subtle variations on his haunting motif. But she had found the lack of any time signature disconcerting at first. Eve finally discovered the secret of playing this music was in listening to her body's own internal rhythm.

But now that she thought of it, since yesterday's accident, that intrinsic cadence had seemed slightly off. Almost as if, as if . . .

"And were your parents originally from here, too?" Sam prodded when Eve went silent on him. He was going to keep their new line of communication open, if he had to ask questions from here to Berkeley and back.

"Oh, my family's lived here for over a century and a half," she offered after only a slight hesitation. "They were mostly fisherman in the early days. From various Scandinavian countries, with a lot of Spanish and Portuguese thrown in from my mother's side to spice up our genetic melting pot. The fishing is why we have that widow's walk on the second floor of the house...so wives and children could watch for returning ships."

"Is that what your father did, fish?" Eve had told him her parents had died recently, but it was about all she had said about them.

"No, he was a lawyer, and for a time, a California state assemblyman," Eve said. Steven, who had political ambitions of his own, had been thrilled with her father's connections.

She had often wondered after their breakup if that had been her only attraction for Steven. Well, he had taken a big chance on losing favor with the good ol' boy network, when he impulsively transferred his affections from one daughter to the other.

But on second thought, maybe not. Steven actually might have increased his stature with the defection, Eve considered cynically. These last couple of decades, politics and playing around seemed to go hand in hand. Or maybe they always had, but in the past the media had just kept quiet about it.

Could it be that driving political ambition was genetically linked to promiscuity?

She looked over at Sam. Perhaps it was just the nature of the male animal. According to Tawny's friend,

Sam had bedded half the feminine population working in the San Diego naval yards. Did that mean he had an elective office in mind for his future? Perhaps with Romancin' Sam, the Ladies' Man, as his slogan?

But somehow, that description just doesn't seem to fit him, Eve found herself thinking, no matter what Tawny's informant had said about his libido. A much more powerful argument about his nature seemed to be the weird set of memories Eve had, in which Amber was alive and Sam didn't even know other women existed . . . sexually, at least.

"And your mother?"

"My mother?"

"What did your mother do? Play the piano?"

"Piano?" she echoed stupidly again, trying to shift mental gears. "No, at least not seriously. Mom was a linguist. She taught Spanish at the language school in Monterey. In fact, my parents were coming back from a week in Guadalajara, Mexico—where my mother had just taken a study group—when my dad's plane crashed."

"I'm sorry, Eve. I really am sorry about your loss."

Yes, he would understand the gaping hole left by the sudden death of a loved one, Eve thought, looking at Sam's taut profile. And she had effectively lost the four most important people in her life last year, almost in one blow.

"Thank you, Sam," she said softly, sending him a wobbly smile. She got one of his gorgeous grins in return. But it was a smile full of the empathy she had sensed between them, almost from the day they had met. Even beyond his obvious physical attraction for her, it was that undeniable bond, which had been so hard for her to break—try as she might—when she had found out he was married.

No! Those were false memories, Eve reminded her addled brain. The truth was that he was a widower... and a footloose, indiscriminate man-about-town. *That* had to be why she had kept him at arm's length and refused to date him... according to what Julie had told her on the phone, half an hour ago.

Wanting to swear at fate for arranging this mess, Eve gave in to the urge to rub her temple instead.

"So, if not your mother, who plays well enough to invest in a concert grand piano and all that music?"

At the sound of Sam's deep voice, Eve quickly dropped her hands to her lap. Worried that he might have seen the telltale gesture and demand that they turn back toward her doctor's office, she replied with a lightheartedness she certainly didn't feel.

"Guilty, as charged." Dancing her fingers over the dashboard, she gave a quick demonstration of her talent by playing along with the Satie composition.

"Are you any good?" Sam challenged with a quick look away from traffic.

Eve bristled, and then suddenly understood he was only trying to take her mind off the deaths of her parents.

"I could have been great," she returned with no false modesty.

"But?"

"But I loved crunching numbers more." She tossed off the answer she had always given to a question many others had asked. However this time Eve heard herself go on. "That's not completely truthful. I do love to play for friends and family... and even for strangers, when I get a job to entertain at a party.

What I couldn't take was the pressure of trying to be a concert pianist.''

"Pressure?'' Sam echoed softly. "What kind of pressure were you under?''

"Oh, there was the need to enter into competition against other pianists, and having to put up with the silly mind games some of them used, trying to psych me out. And if I won, there was all the attention... being the focus of every eye. *That* forced me to attempt more challenging compositions before I had the emotional maturity to really understand them.''

Eve was unable to stop a deep sigh. "My parents were so unhappy when I opted out—when I refused the scholarship to Juilliard—and decided to study math instead. But I was ready to crack. I couldn't live with the pressure anymore... the pressure of being Mom and Dad's perfect daughter!''

Sam didn't know if that startling revelation surprised him or Eve the most. But from the look he saw on her face in a quick glance away from the highway, it was obvious that she had just made a soul-shaking discovery about her childhood... and her parents.

"I'd really like you to play for me sometime, Eve.''

Needing to comfort her, wanting to get that haunted look out of her eyes, Sam had said the first thing that came to mind. And in the silence that followed, he now waited to hear Eve's reaction to his remark.

"Oh... sure, maybe when we get back,'' she finally said in a distracted voice. But then he felt her eyes on his face... and the warmth of her smile. "Or better yet, Julie's nephew is having his Bar Mitzvah next month and I'm playing at the reception. I'm sure she can get you an invitation and a yarmulke.''

Sam laughed in relief... and admiration. Admiration for her strength, for her obvious ability to bounce back from all the blows life had dealt her.

Listening to Sam chuckle at her attempt to lighten the atmosphere, Eve suddenly felt a whole lot better. It was very strange... instead of being embarrassed about telling Sam so much about herself, she just wanted to thank him for the opportunity.

Why hadn't she understood before now that she had been angry at her parents all these years? Why hadn't she recognized that she had resented their pressure... their trying to push her into a career she didn't want?

And somehow, now that she had told Sam about her hidden feelings, Eve understood the subconscious pain they must have been causing her all along. Maybe Sam was wasting his time as a computer security guru. Maybe he should take a crash course in psychology and hang out his shingle.

She sneaked a covert look at his gorgeous profile again. And maybe, Eve thought, maybe *she* could help *him.* Perhaps he also needed a chance to examine his memories... and his own buried anger.

"Hey, Sam. I think it's only fair that I get a round of Twenty Questions with you, now that you've made me spill my guts about my family, and such!"

He looked over at her, one dark eyebrow raised in question. But then he said, "Good enough. Fair is fair... Ask anything you want to know... within reason."

"All right. Tell me.... Oh, here's where we merge with Highway 101. Stay to the left. Birthplace?"

"Huh?"

"My first question. Where were you born, Sam?"

"Uh ... in Detroit ... Michigan."

"Oh, that's right, you told me that during a coffee break one day."

"I did?"

"Yes, I remember ..." Eve hesitated. She did remember the scene perfectly. But she also recalled watching lights glint off of Sam's wedding ring during that conversation. A conversation that could not have happened.

"Eve? Is that it? No more questions?"

"Questions?" A million of them, but none he had answers for. So she rattled off a volley from the top of her head. "Tell me about your family. What is their background and occupations? Do you have any brothers or sisters ... if so, what are their names and ages?"

"Whoa ... one question at a time, Eve," Sam said while he automatically checked his sideview mirror as a long stream of traffic zoomed by. He tried to loosen the death grip his fingers had on the steering wheel, and then concentrate on answering Eve.

"Okay, let's see. My father came from Irish-American stock, and worked in a car factory. My mother's people were Irish, too. She recently got a doctorate in behavioral psychology. And I was their only child."

A true enough summary, Sam thought, as far as it went. But he should have added that during most of his growing-up years, a more accurate description of his family would have been: father, a drunk; mother, an abused wife. And the son? A skinny shrimp until his growth spurt at seventeen. The added inches had come too late to help him physically stop his huge father's violence. By the time he was taller—and stronger—than his father, it hadn't mattered anymore.

What would Eve think of him if he told her the whole story of his childhood? He threw her a quick glance. He had never been able to tell Amber everything. Years of hiding the truth from teachers and friends—everyone—had made it almost impossible for Sam to open up.

Ironically, the navy had been thrilled with his psychological profile. His youth had given him just the qualities needed for someone involved in top secret work.

"Are both your parents still alive?" Eve asked, obviously determined to ask every one of those Twenty Question she had coming to her.

And maybe, since she had trusted him enough to dredge up a painful reality about her own parents, Sam suddenly found it easy enough to answer her...and even to reveal a bit more of himself than he had ever managed before.

"My mom is alive. She moved to Florida last year to take a job at a clinic that specializes in spousal abuse. My dad died when I was sixteen. He was a drunk and a bully. And at the time, I thought his dying was the best thing he ever did for me and my mother."

"Oh, Sam, his problems must have been really hard on you and your mother."

"Well, since he managed to die in an industrial accident, at least there was a bit of insurance money. It paid for some of my education...and my mother's degrees when she decided to go back to school."

"I'm glad something good came from his death," Eve murmured.

"That's exactly what my mother said."

Out of the corner of his eye, Sam watched as Eve's slender fingers reached out to hover over his hand for a heartbeat. But then she pulled back without actually expressing with her touch the sympathy she obviously felt for his long-ago pain.

There were those damned barriers slamming into place again! A vivid picture of roadblocks formed in his mind. Eve constructed them every time he got too close to her emotions.

"Where did you go to high school, Sam? And how did you come to major in computers in college?"

Sam didn't know whether to laugh or curse, once again marveling at Eve's stubborn one-track mind. He wished he had never let her play this wretched game.

"Eve, aren't we pretty close to that question limit?" Sam asked, and then groaned when she shook her head and held up five long, slender fingers. Well, at least all this was taking his mind off driving the freeway, with the traffic whizzing by on his left.

"Okay, okay. Three more, after these two. I went to a public high school on Detroit's west side. When I got to the University of Michigan, I thought about going into geology... like my roommate, Dave. But in the end, computer engineering, with its RAM disks and algorithms, eventually won out over geosynclines and earthquakes."

In the silence that followed his answers, Sam waited for Eve to comment, or come up with her remaining allotment of questions. But she seemed to have lost interest, and was staring out her window.

Eve sat clenching her hands in her lap to keep them from trembling, her eyes turned blindly to the passing countryside. For the last several seconds she had been fighting the sudden wave of fear that had swept over her at Sam's casual reference to geology and earthquakes. From out of nowhere, the vision of devastation caused by her phantom memories replayed in horrible detail in her head.

"Say, Eve, how about digging into that bag you brought and tossing me an apple or something?"

Jolted back from the dark journey her mind was taking, Eve suddenly realized that Sam had asked her a question.

"Oh, sure, just a second," she said belatedly, searching through the paper sack. Her fingers were still shaking when they finally closed around a shape they identified as the large, red apple she had included.

"Here you go, Sam. But if you're really hungry, we could stop in Gilroy up the road. It's the garlic capital of the world, and we could have a dish of their famous garlic ice cream."

"I think I'll pass right now," he said with a startled bark of laughter. "But maybe we can come back another time and try it."

He took a healthy bite out of the apple she had given him, and then devoted all of his attention to chewing it for the next few minutes.

Entranced, Eve sat watching the muscles play on Sam's strong, square jaw. She didn't know why such a simple, everyday action should seem so erotic to her. In self-defense, she forcibly turned her head away to gaze out the side window at passing farmland.

Green acres of artichokes and blue fields of brussels sprouts had been laid out to make a beautifully abstract pattern. The Monterey Peninsula's summers—

cool and foggy—were perfect for these crops. It would be nice if the whole trip were as scenic.

"Don't get to see much of the countryside from the freeway, do you?" Sam commented, pulling her attention back to him when she realized that, once again, he was in sync with her thoughts.

"No... and when I'm not in a hurry, I like to take the old two-lane routes," Eve admitted.

Nodding, Sam reached over to remove the finished Satie tape and insert another.

A glorious, golden reverberation of trumpets filled the car, followed by a majestic theme picked up by the strings and then the woodwinds.

"Oh, Lord," Eve suddenly cried. "I don't know this music. Sam, I've never heard this symphony in my life!"

Chapter Nine

"I'm sorry, Eve, I wasn't paying attention...what did you say?"

"This symphony. It's magnificent, and it has to be Mozart...the style is identical to his. But I can't place it!"

"Well, don't feel bad, he wrote an awful lot of symphonies."

"That's not the point. Sam, I *know* all of Mozart's forty-one symphonies. He's probably my favorite composer. But I've never heard this before."

"He wrote forty-two symphonies, Eve. Look, I don't understand a tenth of what you do about music, but I am familiar with this work. It's Mozart's last symphony—number forty-two—'The Redemption.' You must remember how sick he was before he wrote it. That was when he made his famous vow to God to clean up his act, if he got better. You know, no more wine or women—except for his wife, of course."

"And he also had time to finish his Requiem Mass." Eve made a stabbing guess.

"Right. But a few weeks later he fell off the wine wagon—both literally and figuratively—and died of a concussion."

Eve closed her eyes. So this was what most people experienced—knowledge getting fuzzier and fuzzier with the passage of time. This must be another result of her head injury. Now she was going to spend the rest of her life having to relearn things every few years, just to keep her memory sharp.

Welcome to the rest of the world, Eve. Use it, or lose it, sweetie, that wretched little voice in her head taunted.

"Use it, or lose it," she whispered. She had heard the phrase dozens of times, but never really understood it before. What arrogance! Well, she was getting her just deserts.

Eve pressed her lips together to keep from telling Sam she remembered nothing of the last days of Mozart's life. At least, not the version he had just told her. But if she confessed to him, he'd insist on going right to the nearest hospital for an evaluation.

Which is probably just what I should be doing, Eve thought. And she would, but only after she spoke to Janet. Because, in spite of everything, she felt more and more certain that her sister must leave the city before tomorrow night.

In fact, she found herself pressing an imaginary gas pedal with her foot, almost as if she could will them to get to Berkeley faster.

Looking out the window, Eve saw signs indicating that the next off-ramps were for San Leandro. Glancing at her watch, she determined that they had been on the road for almost three hours. Dammit, they should have been in Berkeley by now. Traffic was heavy, but not that bad.

A huge semi-trailer roared by them in the middle lane, rattling Sam's car in the wind of its passage. It was then Eve noticed they were in the slow lane... moving at fifty-five miles an hour.

Going under the speed limit on a California highway? That was almost unconstitutional! She had been so involved in talking with Sam, it was only now she realized they had been traveling at that velocity for almost the entire trip.

About to ask Sam to speed up, Eve discovered a light sheen of moisture dotting his wide forehead. The tight grip his hands had on the steering wheel made his knuckles gleam whitely. It was obvious that he was tense. In fact, he looked distressed. But he had said he loved to drive.

And he had lied!

Of course, he wouldn't like driving at high speeds. He had probably been doing quite a clip when Amber had been killed.

The wave of sadness sweeping over Eve was so strong, she almost cried out loud. He was doing something he obviously hated, just for her... because of the stupid bump on her head.

What a contradiction he was. How could he be so caring and nurturing toward her, yet so thoughtless of the feelings of all the San Diego women he had bedded and then dumped?

Eve often heard men dismiss their peripatetic lifestyles with the rationalization that they only dated women who "knew the score." Ladies who just wanted a good time and weren't interested in a commitment.

Horse puckey, as her father used to say. Eve had yet to meet a woman who really lived in such a casual manner.

"We have a choice coming up," Sam said, breaking into her disturbing thoughts. "Should I take U.S. 80?"

"Right. I mean, that's correct. We go through the Maze and then get off at the University Avenue exit."

Maze was an apt description for the enormous arches of reinforced concrete roadway curving off in all directions, Eve thought as they whizzed around the twisting ramps.

They were passing through Oakland, and would be in Berkeley in another minute or two. She found herself wondering if any of these overpasses were the ones she had seen fallen and crumbled in her vision of the earthquake.

And after they left the freeway, taking University Avenue eastward, Eve's eyes seemed to superimpose images of collapsed, smoking ruins over the stores and small apartment buildings they passed.

Fighting the need to scream at Sam to go faster, and get them to her sister's place "right now," Eve forced herself to calm down and give him coherent instructions.

"Okay, Sam. I think we're coming up on their street. Stay to the right. Yes, there it is, turn here." She consulted the slip of paper Janet had sent for the exact address. The numbers were the same as those in her head, but Eve just couldn't trust her perfect recall to work anymore.

"I think they're in the next block. It's got to be the apartment right after that truck. Oh, good! There's a parking place in front without a meter."

Slowly getting out of the car, Eve stretched her legs and arms. She felt so tired, and hungry, and scared.

Scared of confronting Janet...and of seeing Steven again.

She was afraid the rift between her and her sister would be even wider after this visit. But remembering the purpose of the trip, she resolutely went up the short flight of stairs to the entry. The door was locked. Eve looked around for a bell.

"Under each mailbox." Sam indicated the row of metal boxes on the wall to the left of the door.

"I wish you wouldn't do that. Read my mind...I mean," Eve complained, her edgy mood making her speak more harshly than Sam's offense warranted.

"Well, sor-ry," he said, with a tug on her ponytail and a grin that took her mind off the reunion with Janet completely.

"What's their last name again?" Sam asked after she had been staring up at him for a long minute.

"Oh!" Eve felt her face flame. "Uh...Lange, I guess."

"Right...Lange. Here it is, apartment 2A." He stabbed the button with a long finger. And then tried it again after a few seconds.

"Damn...don't tell me we've come all this way, and won't be able to talk to them. Is there a building manager indicated?"

"No, but how about a neighbor?" Sam pushed 2B.

"Yes. Who is it?" The tinny voice was barely audible. Sam gestured for Eve to answer.

After checking the identification plate under the apartment number, she complied. "Mrs. Jethrow, my name is Eve Gray. I'm Janet Lange's sister. Do you know when they'll be home?"

"What? Did you say Jerome?"

"No...I said, could you tell us when Janet or Steven Lange will be back?"

"Of course I can. Who's asking?"

"Mrs. Jethrow, I'm Janet's sister. I've driven all the way up from Monterey to see her. Are they away for the weekend? Or will they be home later tonight?"

"Steven said that he'll be back at seven or so, called me this morning, he did. Went on a business trip for his firm, you know. I've been taking care of their cat."

"And what about Janet?" Eve asked, glancing at her watch. It was just after four.

"Oh, I don't think she's coming back."

Did Mrs. Jethrow mean that Janet was going to be out of town for a few more days? Eve hoped so...but if Steven was expected tonight, she still had to warn him.

"Well, if Janet does return, or Steven gets home early, would you tell them I'll be back here at seven o'clock, and to wait for me?"

"What did you say your name was?"

"Eve. Just tell them, Eve."

"Eve. Nice name. Biblical."

"Yes, it is. You'll tell Steven, Mrs. Jethrow?"

"I'll tell him. My sister is picking me up, and we're spending New Year's at her place up north in Chico, but I told Steven I'd wait until he picked up the cat."

"That's very nice of you, Mrs. Jethrow. Have a good time at your sister's. 'Bye."

"Chico's far enough away, if ... anything happens here?" Sam asked when Eve released the speaker button.

She nodded, knowing her relief that Mrs. Jethrow would be safe ... if anything did happen, had been in her voice.

"You're a very caring young woman, sweetheart," Sam said, dropping a light kiss on Eve's nose. "So, what do we do for the next three hours?"

With her blood singing in her veins from just that innocent gesture, Eve fought from telling Sam just exactly how she would like to spend that time with him. But then her stomach saved her, answering Sam's question with the sound of a delicate rumble.

She seconded it anyway. "Eat. And I know a place serving the best pizza this side of Italy!"

"I don't think they have pizza in Italy," Sam said, just to be contrary.

"Then west of New York City," Eve responded equably.

"Right. Shall we drive there?"

"Nah, it's only a mile or so up on Telegraph Avenue. I don't know about you, but I've had enough sitting for a while."

"Me, too." Sam reached up with both hands over his head and gave a big stretch.

Eve found her eyes riveted by the sight of him towering over her. She had never met anyone so much bigger than she was. And for an instant, she was no longer on a residential Berkeley street, but rather in a dimly lit room, stretched out on a huge bed, with Sam poised over her.

His wide shoulders almost blocked out the light, but Eve could see enough to know that in another second he would claim her, brand her body with the fire of his need.

"Okay, lead on, McDuff, I'm starved."

Abruptly turning away from the vision of one kind of hunger, she started off for the pizzeria to sate another. Sam quickly caught up with her and Eve found she had her work cut out for her, trying to match his long-legged stride.

But she soon found a rhythm to match his, and then freed her mind to savor the little fantasy she had indulged in a few moments ago. At least she knew it was only a sensuous daydream . . . a completely normal response to this virile man. The erotic scene in her mind was particularly compelling, because it was not a bogus memory from some other life she had never lived.

RUBIO'S PIZZERIA looked like a typical diner on the outside. But once inside the place, the aroma of pizza perfection hit Sam's nose.

After ordering one with the works, they took cups of coffee to a small table by the window.

"I'm going to scout out the bathroom," Eve announced, depositing her cup on the Formica-topped surface.

"Yeah, I'm for that, too. But you go first and I'll guard our territory." He indicated the crowd that had built up while they were ordering and was now looking for seats.

When Eve returned from freshening up, Sam was deep into reading the San Francisco *Chronicle*.

"Hi. Want to look at this? Someone left the morning edition on the windowsill." Sam got up and handed the paper to Eve.

"Oh, great, but I just want the sports section."

"So, you're a sports fan?"

"Addict. At least to football. What's your favorite team?"

"Well, truthfully, I don't have one anymore. I used to root for the Detroit Lions, but since leaving Michigan . . . Well, I hate to say it, but I couldn't tell you much about any of the teams or their players now."

"Then what were you so engrossed in when I came back?"

"The comics. Check out 'Doonesbury' and 'Garfield,' they're terrific today." Sam laughed and made for the rest room.

Eve found herself still smiling while she turned to the sports section. She scanned the headlines, and then, using them as a test, she looked at the statistics listed on the third page. Closing her eyes, she tried to recall what she had just read. The columns of numbers popped into place in her mind's eye and, like a computer screen, the scores scrolled down behind her lids.

Checking the originals, Eve confirmed they were exactly the same. Maybe the unsettling side effects caused by the blow to her head were wearing off. Eve tried the experiment twice more before Sam returned, and she remembered the scores perfectly each time.

Feeling much more optimistic that she would soon recover her memory of the real events that had occurred to her during the last few weeks, Eve was able to do justice to the delicious pizza.

"Well, we've killed forty-five minutes," Sam announced, patting his absolutely flat stomach. "Where to now, Eve?"

"Why don't we walk off some of these calories and see what crazy new developments have taken place on Telegraph Avenue since the last time I was here."

Out on the street once more, they strolled northward, toward the University of California campus. A few blocks south of the college grounds the sidewalks were clogged with students and tourists. Adding to the congestion were the dozens of handicraft stands vendors had set up near the curbs on each side of the street.

Surging around the booths were people whom Eve always thought were more interesting and varied than the goods being offered for sale.

Sam seemed to think so, too. She watched with secret amusement while his head snapped around when they passed sitar players in flowing robes. A little farther up the avenue she smiled at his reaction to a couple in beads and buckskin, who were apparently still lost in the sixties.

And when they crossed Haste Street, she barely kept from laughing out loud as Sam studiously avoided even glancing at the ladies dressed in minuscule leather skirts and skinny high heels, plying an ancient trade.

But Eve didn't find it funny when a phalanx of spiked-haired skinheads advanced on them. Sam suddenly put his arm around her shoulders, pulling her closer to his hard body.

The grim scowl on his face and the penetrating warning in his eyes were enough to make the approaching men close up ranks and pass them by with plenty of sidewalk room to spare.

Surprisingly, Eve found herself secretly thrilled by Sam's protective male response. Every primitive female instinct in her body demanded she be pleased because this big, strong male was looking out for her.

Her feminist friends from university days would have run her out of town for admitting to those atavistic feelings. Yet, Eve was finding it hard to go against a million years of natural selection.

It's just too bad Sam doesn't qualify for that other ancient goal of womankind, Eve told herself. He most certainly was *not* a monogamous man who would invest himself in only her and their children.

Her lighthearted mood abruptly evaporated. Eve managed a graceful release from Sam's grasp when she stopped and carefully examined a display of spun-glass novelties offered by a street merchant.

"See anything you'd like to have?" Sam whispered into her ear a few minutes later.

Just you.

The words fought to be free of censoring lips. But Eve forced herself to keep her mouth shut and eyes focused on the items in front of her. She didn't dare let Sam look at her face to see the longing that must still linger there. He was too damned good at reading her mind, by half!

"Oh, no... nothing," she finally mumbled. "Let's check out the other tables."

Eve hurriedly moved to a stand selling hand-made silver buckles and jewelry. A group of Japanese tourists crowded around her and Sam. The cameras hanging around their necks bounced every which way as they avidly searched for the finest specimens.

Taking a step back to get away from the jostling, Eve suddenly noticed a man brandishing a sign on the other side of the road. He reminded her of the street prophets in innumerable Sunday comics.

Shop Now... For The World Will End Tomorrow! this one seemed to proclaim.

Rubbing her eyes, Eve felt a wave of relief when she read the poster a second time.

Shop Nathan's... For Our Year-End Sale Tomorrow!

But looking at the hundreds of people around her, Eve abruptly wondered if, like Chicken Little, she shouldn't be marching up and down here with a placard of her own, warning everyone to get out of town because the Big One was coming.

Shaking off the sense of panic her errant memories were producing, she checked on Sam, who was still looking at the belt buckles. Eve wandered over to the next table.

This stand sold jewelry of all kinds. One of the items, a ring fashioned into a circle of golden conch shells, immediately caught her attention. She found herself staring at it, suddenly swaying, as if the earthquake had hit a day early and the sidewalk was rocking beneath her feet.

Amber! This was just the kind of jewelry Amber had created and worn to the New Year's party of her phantom memories! Eve swung around, ready to drag Sam over here and show him the proof...

But proof of what? A dream? A nightmare?

SAM LOOKED UP and found Eve staring at him. His heart kicked into a quicker rhythm, and he unconsciously moved to close the space between them. He was about to take Eve's hand when he saw her attention had shifted away from him to focus on the table in front of her. His eyes were captured by a glint of precious metal.

Standing stock-still, Sam stared at the small circle of golden shells laying on black velvet. Amber's work...he was sure of it! How had it come to be here, eight thousand miles and three years away from her death in Australia?

Picking up the delicate ring, he used the last of the day's light to look inside and verify that her registered trademark was etched there: a beautifully stylized *AG*. Amber Goodman, her maiden name.

She had planned to officially change her logo to *AD,* but there had not been the time nor the need. Amber had never created another piece of work after pledging her vows to him. He had killed her before she could.

Holding the ring tightly in his fist, Sam closed his eyes, debating what to do about it. Should he buy it, as his first impulse demanded? Or should he leave it so someone else could enjoy his wife's artistry?

His *first* wife. Loved—cherished—but gone. Placing the ring carefully back on its bed of velvet, Sam blindly walked away from the realization that he had just said a final farewell to Amber.

Farewell, and godspeed.

A sixth sense learned in football days kept his wide shoulders from doing serious damage to people as his feet plowed up the street.

He finally stopped at another stand glittering cheerfully in the streetlights that had just popped on. Nothing of Amber's work here . . . just row upon row of dainty filigreed earrings. Jewelry that would look beautiful dangling from Eve's ears.

Eve . . . the woman he had wanted at first sight, and probably was in love with by their second meeting.

Eve!

Swiveling around, Sam didn't see her at first. Only when she moved from the protection of a doorway, did he locate her tall, slender presence. She was looking at him, a thin line of worry marring the smooth sweep of her brow.

He held a hand out to her, and there was only a slight hesitation on her part before she walked to him.

Taking her exquisitely formed fingers in his palm, Sam closed his hand around hers, lifting it to brush his lips against the smooth skin of her knuckles. He tried to silently convey to her with the gesture that he was all right... and if she were by his side, he would always be all right.

Taking the fact that she didn't pull her hand away as an agreement with his thoughts, Sam turned to the vendor, who was hovering over his wares.

"Sir, let's see that pair of earrings on this end, third row down," Sam directed.

"Oh, no, please don't," Eve protested when he held the jet and emerald-colored baubles up to her ears. She objected even more strenuously when he handed over the required amount of money to the artisan.

"They suit you," he said, brushing aside her continued arguments.

"But... but..."

"Put them on, Eve. I want to see them on you."

And one day, he wanted to see what they would look like when she wore nothing else. That, however, would have to wait. Wait until Eve accepted that what they felt for each other was right, and true, and meant to be.

Something of his thoughts must have penetrated the renewed barriers Eve had placed between them before starting on this trip. She finally took the earrings and inserted the metal wires into her pierced ears.

"Thank you, Sam. They're beautiful."

Sam smiled down at her. The earrings somehow transformed her face from beautiful to mysteriously exotic.

"Excuse me, folks, if there's nothing else you'd like, I'll be closing up for today."

Turning to look at the vendor and then around the street, Sam realized the crowds had thinned and most of the sidewalk merchants were putting away their wares.

"It's only six-fifteen," Eve said with a glance at her watch, and then at the used bookstore behind them. "Want to go inside here for a few minutes? They've got a terrific selection of science fiction I can't resist rummaging through whenever I'm in town."

"Sounds great, lead the way," Sam said, gratified to see a happy light back in her eyes.

Inside the shop, the slightly musty, wonderfully evocative scent of thousands of old books hit Eve's nose. Grinning with anticipation, she wove her way through a labyrinth of high, tightly packed bookshelves. At the back of the store, she located the rather rickety staircase leading up to the second floor and the store's collection of science fiction.

As always, feeling that she was gaining entrance to a rare treasure trove when she climbed these steps, Eve carefully negotiated her way to the top.

There had been little attempt up here to put order to the chaos of books that filled every corner. Eve suspected the store's owners knew about the secret thrill their customers experienced when a search through the precariously balanced volumes yielded unexpected riches.

At least, Eve always felt the plunder discovered in this way was more valuable, because it was the result of her patient digging. Feeling like an archaeologist who had come upon an unsullied tomb, Eve happily began her random searchings.

She was only vaguely aware that Sam—grinning as he surveyed his surroundings—rubbed his hands together in obvious anticipation, and then went to the other side of the room on his own expedition.

A quarter hour into her hunt, Eve let out a muffled whoop of triumph when she encountered a thin paperback novel identical to the one she had loaned Sam last night.

Sarban's *The Sound of His Horn*.

Eve was about to call Sam over and present him with her discovery, when she noticed another volume under the first book that had a similar illustration on the cover.

Holding up her new find to the light, Eve saw it was another novel by Sarban called *The Roar of the Lion*. A quick scan of the back cover revealed it to be a sequel to the first story she held in her other hand. It was also a title she had never heard of before.

With a sudden shudder, Eve closed her eyes, waiting for the now familiar wave of strangeness to crest in her mind.

Perhaps, since it had happened so often in the past twenty-four hours, the impact of this discovery was not so bad this time. Taking a deep breath, she decided not to worry why there should be a fifth Sarban book here, when she knew the author had only published four works of fiction in his lifetime.

This was just another fact to add to the growing weight of information her brain was gathering. Sam's reaction out on the street to the ring she had thought might have been crafted by Amber had also gone into the heap.

Somewhere, deep in her mind, Eve felt a faint stirring. A rearranging of information molecules was taking place in there. She knew what was happening. It was similar to the process she had experienced in her advanced math and statistics classes.

A seemingly impossible problem was being examined by her subconscious. In the gray matter of her brain, where her mathematical talents lay, a solution cooked. Her analytic mind would eventually present her with an answer to every weird thing that had occurred to her since meeting Sam.

So, a few minutes later, when it was time to leave, Eve just took the new novel to the cashier, along with the other volume. Not letting Sam see what she had purchased for him, Eve slipped the package into her purse and followed the tall man out into the night.

Standing on the darkened street, she was again assaulted by the eerie feeling her time was running out. Eve couldn't help the compulsive urge to look at her watch. Ten to seven.

"Sam, I guess we should go and see if my sister or her husband has gotten home yet."

Although she was dreading the coming encounter, Eve was somehow glad Sam would be at her side when she saw Janet and Steven for the first time in almost a year.

"I'm with you all the way," Sam murmured in another demonstration of how he could pick up on her thoughts.

They quickly walked back to her sister's street in the penetrating cold that had settled on the city. Eve was freezing by the time they reached the apartment building, although she didn't know if her hands were so icy because of the lowering temperature or from the case of nerves that had shudders skittering up and down her spine.

At the top of the stairs, Eve took a deep breath, and rang the little bell under the Lange nameplate.

Chapter Ten

"Eve? Why are you here? Have you seen Janet, yet? What did she tell you?"

Sounding like a prosecuting lawyer in the case of *Lange v. Gray*, Steven had begun interrogating Eve the moment he opened his apartment door.

"Janet wasn't here when we stopped by earlier, Steven," Eve answered, surprised at how steady her voice was. "I haven't spoken to her."

"No, of course, she wouldn't have been here. Well, come in, come in," he offered with a sweeping gesture of his hand.

Eve had forgotten just how handsome Steven was, how perfectly chiseled his features. With his thick blond hair and vivid blue eyes, he looked like a storybook prince. Of course, she knew very well that a slimy frog dwelt inside his noble facade.

He must have just gotten home, Eve thought. He was still wearing a dark blue suit, the maroon silk tie knotted tight over a blindingly white shirt. A power outfit. Yet, somehow, he didn't look very impressive to her. Perhaps that was because of the truly imposing man standing at her side.

"Oh, Sam, sorry. This is Steven Lange," Eve offered belatedly. "My... sister's husband. Steven, this is Sam Davidson. He works at the same facility I do."

Steven held out his hand. "Ah, glad to meet you, Sam."

Eve watched Sam look speculatively at the well-manicured hand outstretched toward himself. Towering over Steven, Sam projected an aura of dangerous alertness, as if he had picked up on her unease and was waiting for Steven to make the slightest misstep. He eventually gave his fingers a short, powerful squeeze.

"Why don't you both sit down?" Steven offered with visible reluctance after that handshake. "Can I get you two anything to drink? Eat?"

"No, we're fine." Sam answered for the both of them, which—for reasons Eve didn't want to analyze at the moment—suited her perfectly.

From her location on a plush two-seater couch, Eve looked around for the first time. She discovered the apartment was one giant room, with areas demarked for entertaining and eating. A metal staircase curved upward to a cantilevered platform that must be a sleeping loft, now closed off by a set of huge accordion doors.

"Quite a bit classier than my old place, huh, Eve? Even has a real stove and a bed big enough..." Steven stopped short, reddening when he seemed to remember just whom he was trying to impress.

His jilted fiancée, the woman he had thrown over for her sister.

A second later a loud mew split the silence that had fallen in the room. Eve turned to see a huge calico cat come out from the kitchen area. Surveying the humans who had invaded her territory, she stalked forward and made a graceful leap into Sam's lap. "Jezebel, get down from there!" Steven shouted at the feline.

"That's all right, I like cats," Sam said, stroking behind the animal's ears after she had made two turns and settled across his thighs.

"Sorry, she's usually very standoffish. Dump Jezebel anytime you get tired of her," Steven said before turning back to Eve.

Steven's philosophy toward females, in a nutshell, she thought ruefully.

"I just picked up Jezebel from the neighbor you talked to, Mrs. Jethrow. I was down in L.A. for the firm. They've been sending me all over the country. Working sixty-hour weeks, but it's paying off," he boasted, gesturing to the apartment again.

"Well, I'm glad you're able to provide so well for Janet." Not interested in further small talk, Eve decided to get to the matter at hand. "Steven, I was glad to receive the Christmas card you and Janet sent."

Actually, since Eve couldn't remember getting the greeting, she had no idea *how* she'd felt...but she was not going to reveal that to Steven...or remind Sam of the fact. She glanced at the man next to her. His long, strong fingers were still gently stroking Jezebel. The calico's eyes were half-closed in ecstasy. Lucky cat.

"Yes, lovely design, wasn't it?"

Steven's comment pulled Eve back from the image of herself curled on Sam's lap, purring while those fingers caressed her own skin.

"Janet spent a long time on the painting. She wanted it to be right. And since you're here, I guess it worked. The card said just what both of us meant. We're sorry that we caused you *any* pain."

"It was a horrible time, anyway. Even without . . . what happened between . . . us," Eve said, not wanting to dwell on those dark days.

She glanced at Sam again. His hand had stopped its stroking motion. He sat absolutely still, his face closed and unreadable.

He's probably embarrassed at having to listen to my personal problems, she thought. Eve was about to suggest he might want to wait in the car when Steven spoke again.

"Eve, has Janet contacted you?"

"Well, yes . . . the card."

"No, I mean since then? It happened after she sent you that Christmas greeting."

"What happened? Steven, what's wrong? What's going on here?"

"She's left me, Eve. Janet's gone, and she's filing for divorce."

"Left you? Divorce? Steven, what—"

"I was stupid, that's what. Stupid and immature. Not thinking past the whim of the moment."

"You cheated on her," Eve whispered, certain she was right, suddenly remembering all the agony this man had helped cause her last year.

"Yeah. But, Eve, it didn't mean anything. Not really."

"It never did. I didn't, either, did I? Not before we were engaged, or after."

Eve vaguely heard the sharp intake of air into Sam's lungs, but her attention remained focused on Steven.

Steven appeared to have forgotten about Sam, too. "Eve, when Janet came home for your parents' funeral, I couldn't help myself. I fell in love with her the moment I met her at the airport. And after you found us together, I tried to tell you how it was. I called and wrote—"

"Steven. I probably would have given you two my blessing, if you had just come to me before...what happened. It was the order of events that made it all so sordid." Eve didn't dare look at Sam. But she felt the heat—the anger—radiating from his body.

The cat had obviously felt it, too. With a loud hiss, Jezebel abruptly jumped to the carpet and raced up the spiral staircase to the loft above.

"Eve..." Steven began.

"Look, Steven, let's just say what happened was the best for me in the long run. But apparently not for Janet. There seems to be a pattern here. How did Janet find out? Did you seduce a friend of hers? Like you tried with Cathy and Sara Ann? They told me you—"

"Your roommates? They told you? Well that explains why you stayed so distant, even after we got engaged."

"Distant? How can you say I was distant?" Eve shook her head, remembering how she had exploded at her roommates when they warned her Steven had made passes at each of them, and urged her to think long and hard about marrying him.

"Eve, at least there wasn't any real harm done. After what your roommates told you, and then your parents' deaths, there never..."

"Steven, it's over and done with. You're right. No permanent damage was done. I've survived. As far as what you took from me, well, I'll chalk it up to my own bad judgment."

"Eve, I'm not sure..." Steven began.

"Look, I came up here because your answering machine was full," Eve interrupted, getting to her feet a second before Sam did. "I wanted to invite Janet to a party, tomorrow. We're having a big New Year's bash at the facility. I'd like her—both of you—to come down to Monterey for it. Would you please tell my sister it's very important to me for her to be there?"

"Eve, I'd love to go to your party with Janet, but I've been trying to tell you—I don't know where she is!" The pain and worry in his voice was obvious, even to Eve. "Janet's given her lawyer instructions not to reveal her whereabouts or phone number to me, or anyone. I've left a dozen messages with the woman, and Janet hasn't answered one of them."

"Not answered?" Eve felt dizzy. All this way and she couldn't warn Janet? "Can I have the lawyer's number?"

"Sure..." Steven took out his wallet and searched through the sections. "Here's her card. Susan Cohn. Take it, I have more."

"Thank you. Can I use your phone to call now?" Eve glanced at her watch. Almost eight. "Shoot, it's probably too late." She made the call, anyway, leaving a short message—along with her name and Monterey phone number—when the complicated phone mail system finally offered her that option.

After putting down the receiver, she joined Sam at the entry. She looked up at him. "I'll try again first thing in the morning."

He nodded and opened the door.

"Eve!" Steven called as she started down the stairs. "Eve, tell Janet that I love her... and to please come back home. Tell her I'll never hurt her again."

Looking up into Steven's anguish-filled eyes, Eve nodded, and then hurried down the stairs in a haze of worry about how to contact Janet. She didn't even notice Sam following a step behind her, until he unlocked the passenger side of his car.

"That guy is a slimy piece of work," he muttered after he got behind the wheel.

"Steven? Well, he's no prince." Eve shrugged. "But he's probably no worse than most men."

"You think most men are unfaithful to their women?"

"Oh, Sam, don't give me that innocent act." Eve could hear the venom in her voice and vaguely knew she was transferring her rage at Steven onto this man's dark head.

No! Somehow, she was equally angry with Sam. Maybe more. What Julie had told her about his playboy reputation in San Diego echoed in her mind, blotting out her own feelings for him. How dare he have so little regard for women in general, that he could take and take and take from them, without any thought for their feelings? And how dare he jerk *her* emotions around like a yo-yo?

"Oh, I don't know what went on during your marriage," she said icily, "but you haven't set any records for fastidiousness in the past year, have you?"

"What in the hell do you mean?"

"San Diego, Sam. That's what I mean."

"Eve, calm down. You're not making sense. Is your head bothering you?"

"Don't give me that, Sam. I know what happened in San Diego, when you were working in the naval facility."

"What happened? Please tell me what happened, so we'll both know."

"You slept your way through half the female population there, that's what."

"I did what?" His mouth hung open in apparent amazement.

"You went out with dozens of women...bedded each of them a few times, and then dumped them. And if you don't think it mattered because you weren't married, well you're wrong, buster. All those women had feelings...feelings you trampled on. Just like Steven trampled on mine...and now Janet's..."

Eve turned away from Sam, staring out the window at the rows of neat apartment buildings lining the street. The sudden thought of these structures falling into rubble tomorrow night drained away her anger. It was replaced with a sense of hopeless dread.

"Oh, Sam," Eve whispered. "What if I can't find her? You don't know how clear those visions of the earthquake are. I just can't believe it didn't happen. I mean...that it won't happen, tomorrow night."

"Eve, come here, sweetheart." Sam reached across the wide seat, but Eve cringed toward the door. "No, no, don't be afraid of me. I just want to hold you. Nothing more."

When she didn't have the strength, or desire, to protest again, he gathered her into his arms, tucking her head onto his wide shoulder. And with that tender gesture, Eve felt a mental dam break, releasing in a deluge of tears all the emotional pain she had been keeping behind it for the past year.

When the flood ended, Sam fished a clean white handkerchief from his jacket pocket and handed it to Eve. After she wiped away the remaining tears and blew her nose, he pushed back the pale hair that had fallen over her eyes, and ran his fingers down her soft, soft cheek.

"Eve, can you listen to me now and let me put in a word for my defense?" he asked simply.

She nodded, blowing her nose again, looking up at him with such a helpless, lost expression, that Sam groaned out loud.

"Oh, Eve... I'm so sorry for all the sorrow you've endured from that jackass Steven. And for any pain I've caused you, even inadvertently. But I want you to know I am *not* like that guy. I was faithful to Amber for the year we dated and were engaged. And for the twenty-four hours we were married," he added with more than a trace of bitterness.

"But after she died, I was full of anger and guilt. She paid with her life because I turned left instead of right when a drunken driver barreled into us. I had always sworn to myself that when I married, I would protect my wife, with my life if necessary. But I failed to keep that vow. And afterward, when I wanted to die with her, I couldn't even do that. All my years of religious training kicked in, and I couldn't even do that."

Eve stirred in his arms and pulled back to look at his face. "Sam, last year, when my parents died, and I effectively lost my sister as well, I felt I couldn't go on either. But a friend of my dad's, Father Moreno, told me a simple saying that helped me push aside those thoughts. He said to me, 'The loss of even one drop of water makes the sea less blue.'"

"He sounds like one very wise man. I certainly know that my life is an emptier place because Amber's not in it. For the first couple of years after her death, I tried to fill the void by burying myself in work and graduate school classes. By the time I completed my second tour of duty, and mustered out of the navy, I had earned my master's degree. That qualified me to take the job in San Diego as a civilian employee.''

Sam shifted in his seat. So much rested on what he said next. Buying a little time, he ran his hand through his hair and then took a deep breath.

''Eve, it is true that in the year I worked in San Diego, I did go out with a lot of women. I guess I was tired of being so numb... so cold. Cold as the grave. So I looked for a little warmth in my life.''

Sam shook his head and sighed deeply again. ''You were right in this much, at the time, I couldn't deal with intense feelings and emotions. Neither mine nor those of the women I dated. So I never took anyone out more than once or twice... to a dinner, a concert. I knew if I got any more involved than that, it would just hurt them... and me.''

''You mean, you were searching for... warmth, and none of them gave it to you?''

''No, darling, I meant that *I* didn't have anything to give them. Eve, I didn't even *try* to bed any of those ladies. It wouldn't have been fair to anyone involved.''

''But Julie said that Tawny said that her friend Victoria said—''

Sam laughed out loud at the runaway sentence, easing some of the tension he had been under. But then he stopped chuckling and the gruff sound that came from his throat did not convey amusement.

''Ah, Victoria. So now we know the reason for all of this... Victoria Sommers. Eve, I don't know how to prove to you I'm telling the truth, especially after your ex-fiancé hurt you so badly. But Victoria bore absolutely no resemblance to the women I dated in San Diego. Let's just say that she was a classic case of a woman scorned. Victoria began spreading malicious rumors, and she finally went too far and got fired.''

Eve found herself trying to see what lay beyond the deep blue color of Sam's eyes. He was right, she had absolutely no way of knowing whether he was telling the truth or not. But in her gut, she felt he was.

In her month's worth of illusory memories of the ''married'' Sam Davidson, she remembered how he behaved with every woman at the facility, including herself. He had been cheerful, friendly, and nothing more.

Somehow, the power of those defective memories was so forceful, Eve had to accept them. ''I do believe you, Sam,'' she whispered, and a wave of rightness, of peace, settled over her.

''Thank God,'' he said hoarsely. ''Then where do we go from here, Eve?''

Such a simple question, with such a wide range of possible answers. But Eve, knowing her emotions had been strained to the limit, decided to take the only option she was capable of handling at the moment.

Looking at her watch, she saw it was a little after eight. ''Home, Sam. I guess we should go back to Monterey.''

''Coward,'' he said with an affectionate smile. But then his face got serious and his big hands took hold of her shoulders. ''Eve, can I make a confession to you?''

''Sure,'' she agreed a bit apprehensively, not knowing what might be coming next.

"Since Amber died, I've hated driving on free-ways, especially at night."

"Is that how she died, on a highway, at night?"

"Yes."

"Do you want me to drive to Monterey? It's not very late, we'd be back before midnight."

"No, I still don't think you driving right now is a good idea. Not after that hit on your head."

"So...you want us to stay here until tomorrow morning? Rent a room?"

"Rooms. I'm not trying to rush you or take advantage, Eve. We've got all the time in the world now to get to know each other better before we take that wonderful next step."

The sincerity in his voice abruptly breached the fortress of caution Eve had built around herself since her engagement ended. All at once, she felt strong—ready to handle anything. Even a night with Sam!

"Room, Sam. Let's make it one room. Because I *definitely* want to take advantage of you."

THERE WASN'T A WINDOW in the Maritime Hotel that had a bad view. The building hugged the marina, with half its rooms facing the hills of Berkeley, while the other side of the four-storied building looked upon a wonderful panorama of San Francisco, and the two massive bridges linking the city with the East and North Bay communities.

Eve and Sam didn't need an escort to their bay-view room on the fourth floor. Their only luggage consisted of the goodie bag Eve had brought from home and the sack of essentials she bought in the hotel drugstore while Sam arranged for the room.

"Lord, it's a suite," Eve gasped at the sight of the large living area they had walked into. "Sam...this is going to cost us a fortune. But I think it's going to be worth it!"

Dancing in ahead of him, she plopped her purse on a table and then ran to check out their accommodations. One wall of the living area was covered by draperies. Eve decided to evaluate the view in a minute. Swinging around, she crossed the floor to peek through a set of double doors...at the bedroom.

Detouring from that area when butterflies took sudden flight in her stomach, she did a ninety-degree turn and walked through another set of doors leading into a large dressing area. Mirrored closets flanked her to the left and right, while double wash basins at the end of the room were bisected by yet another door.

It turned out to open into a luxurious bathroom with a step-in marble tub, another sink, and a commode, all with gold-plated fixtures. Pirouetting back through the dressing area, Eve saw herself in the mirrored closet doors and gasped.

Reflected over and over by the parallel arrangement of the glass, she saw the naked truth...she was a mess! Her hair looked as though it had barely survived a tornado, her makeup was long gone, and her clothing had wrinkles. Even the wrinkles had wrinkles!

"I'm going to camp out in the bathroom for a few minutes, Sam. Do you need to use it before me?"

"Yeah...be right out," he said, walking past her and dropping a kiss on her bird's-nest hair before going inside.

With her heart tripping in reaction to that innocent gesture, Eve found herself shivering at the thought of what this night would bring her: the culmination of a month of longing...the embrace of the man she loved. Smiling at the multitude of reflections in the mirrors, she turned to go back into the living room. And then stopped.

That feeling she had experienced in the bookstore returned again. Another piece of the puzzle had just been added to the equation her brain was working on. What the final answer would be, she had no idea. All she could do was wait until her mind presented her with its solution. Tied up with a big red ribbon...logical and complete.

Back in the living room she gathered up her purse and took out some of the articles she had bought downstairs in the drugstore. Eve was ready to slip into the bathroom the second Sam came out.

FINISHED washing up in one of the dressing room's marble-shelled sinks, Sam grinned. Eve was so sweetly transparent. She was absolutely terrified of spending their first night together, yet courageously game to go through with it.

Come to think of it, he was pretty scared himself. So much rested on the next few hours in each other's arms.

But he swore he would make sure everything was perfect for this, their first lovemaking. He would take things slow, and not do anything that would give her pause for even a second of concern.

Drying his hands and face, Sam dragged a comb through his hair, and then went into the living room. He lowered the lights and pulled open the drapes. He was standing there, looking out over the Bay, when Eve slipped her arm around his waist.

He immediately placed his own arm around her shoulders and pulled her closer to his side so they could both look out the window.

The view was incredible. San Francisco was ablaze with lights. The illumination on several world-famous skyscrapers had turned them into Art Deco displays. On the city's freeways, speeding cars created sinuous rivers of red and white. And bracketing the central extravaganza were the two luminous bridges, looking as if frolicking fireflies had taken up residence in their supporting girders.

"No wonder San Francisco gets voted the most romantic city in the world over and over again," Eve breathed.

Sam turned Eve in his arms and tilted her chin up. "It's more than beautiful, Eve. But we could be standing in a cold, dripping cave, a mile below the earth, and I'd still feel the same about tonight. Look at my hands, sweetheart . . . I'm shaking like a grass-green boy at the thought of holding you in my arms and making you mine. I'm so in love with you, Eve. And nothing matters more to me, than making you happy tonight and for the rest of our lives."

"Oh, Sam. Oh, Sam," Eve managed to whisper before he sealed his pledge with his mouth, his hands buried deeply in the thick mane of hair she had brushed free for his pleasure.

The burning of his lips, of his seeking tongue, sent fire rushing through every vein. Her answering response caused Sam to moan...a deep, primitive sound that thrilled every feminine cell in Eve's body.

"Are you sure this is what you want, sweetheart?" Sam implored when he finally pulled his mouth off hers to end the sensual devastation of that kiss.

"Damn fool question for me to ask right now, isn't it?"

"Darling, oh, my darling. Don't you know that you're all I've thought about since the moment I first saw you?" Eve said, knowing it was time for her to open her heart and let Sam see just how much she loved him.

"No, I didn't have an inkling. How could I, when you were so cool, even from the day we met? I didn't realize what kind of opinion you already had of me..."

"Opinion? Oh...you mean that Tawny must have told me about San Diego before I met you...for the first time..." Eve replied vaguely. She didn't want to tell Sam that what she really remembered about their first formal meeting was the glint of his wedding ring. It was a false memory...as she had learned today, but the only one she had!

Sam's mouth instantly returned to hers. Open to the welcoming thrust of his tongue, Eve tasted his very essence, and she suddenly knew that she would never get enough of this addictive nectar.

With a groan, Sam turned her in his arms and, never really breaking contact with her lips, led Eve into the bedroom.

Once inside the door, she was vaguely aware of the massive furnishings, and that a door wall opened out onto a narrow balcony. But as he sat down with her on the edge of the king-size bed dominating the room, most of Eve's senses were involved in learning everything she could about Sam.

She found that his thick hair felt like satin, and his strong jaw was like warm marble. And when her mouth nuzzled against the soft skin along the column of his powerful neck, Eve realized that his morning shaving ritual must include a liberal dusting of fresh-smelling baby powder!

A threatening giggle turned into a gasp of pleasure when Sam's hands went under her sweater and began moving over the silk shirt he encountered there. His fingers brushed the fabric until her nipples grew tight and hard.

Somehow, she managed to open Sam's own shirt. Finding the wide, smooth expanse of his chest, Eve laid her cheek against it, listening to the strong beat of his heart. This heart belonged to her, she suddenly exalted! Just as hers belonged to Sam. They had always been meant for each other . . . and now they were finally together.

Looking up to see Sam's dark blue eyes gazing down at her face, Eve smiled. She tried to put all of what she was feeling for him into that smile.

The gentle touch of his fingers against her lips told Eve that Sam had understood. She brushed her mouth against those fingers, against the hard skin of his palm. And then, with a saucy grin, she moved so that her lips and tongue could reach male nipples, which immediately hardened into tiny pebbles. But when her hands traveled down his chest, and tried to open his belt buckle, Sam stopped her fumbling attempts.

"Eve. Please, I'm too close to the edge right now for you to touch me. Let me undress you first. I need to see all of you," he confessed, tugging on the hem of her sweater. Sam lifted it and her silk blouse over her head. He tossed them on a nearby chair, and then, as if unable to resist, trailed his hands over her breasts on the way to the bra's fastener on her back.

With that wisp of lace gone, his fingers came back to linger, to learn the shape and weight of her breasts, until Eve writhed under his touch.

"Damn, this isn't helping my control at all," he grated. Sitting back a bit on the bed, his eyes implored her to finish her own disrobement.

Eve tried to comply. But even as she stood to slip off her slacks and the silken bikini panties that were her remaining cover, one word seemed to shout in her head.

Amazon!

It was the hurtful description Janet had flung at her last year; the cruel label Steven had pinned on his discarded fiancée.

She fought the sudden urge to curl into a ball, to somehow hide her body from Sam. Would he also think there was too much of her...curves, height...everything?

But Sam is not Steven, Eve reminded herself. And with that certainty in her heart, she tossed back her long mane of blond hair...and stood tall.

Let Sam see that I'm wearing only the beautiful earrings he bought for me tonight...and nothing else.

To her surprise, he was gazing into her eyes, and not at her body!

"Eve, my love...I'll always remember this moment. Nothing has ever meant more to me than this gift you're making of your heart and soul."

"Oh, Sam. They're yours...they have always been yours," Eve cried, sinking down next to him onto the bed, because her knees were unable to hold her up under the sweet, heavy burden of his words.

In swift, economical motions, Sam shed his own clothing.

Eve only had the most fleeting glimpse of him when he turned back to her. Even so, that brief instant caused her breath to catch in her throat.

But then he took her into his arms and brought her with him, to lay fully stretched out on the bed. They pressed together as closely as possible, fused from shoulder to toe. And, somehow, Eve no longer felt afraid.

Instead, she wanted to explore every part of Sam, to know each and every magnificent inch of his body. But there was no time. She needed him too badly. She needed him to be part of her.

Eve felt as if waiting another second for his possession would put her in danger of losing Sam forever. She feared that he would slip away from her, as he had done in all her midnight fantasies.

"Sam, please..."

"You're not ready, Eve," he argued. But when his hands cupped her breasts and she felt his lips and tongue on her nipples, Eve felt stabbing pleasure flash down into the deepest part of her being.

A few minutes—or an eternity later—he murmured, "Is it time, now?" when he finally directed his touch to the site of her greatest need.

"Sam!"

"Yes, now, my love."

When he moved over her, Eve gladly opened to Sam's stormy invasion. The first silken press of him was all she needed to fly over the edge of passion into a free-falling swirl of incredible pleasure.

But in the next instant, a searing white flash of pain and confusion tore into the pinnacle of her ecstasy. Her body instinctively clenched in reaction to the intensity of Sam's movements as he neared his own completion.

When it came, Eve could only ride the whirlwind of his release, her eyes riveted to his face. With her name torn from deep within his chest, he threw back his head as his frame shuddered again and again.

Eve automatically wrapped her arms around his wide shoulders when he collapsed on her. He pressed his cheek on hers, and then gently rubbed it against her skin. The rough stubble of new growth made a faint rasp, until the lubricating moisture generated by sweat . . . or tears . . . muffled the sound.

"Oh, sweetheart." Sam sighed. He reluctantly moved his weight off of Eve's slender body, but immediately needed to gather her back into his arms. "Never . . . never have I felt anything like this."

And it was true. With Eve, he had been able to ride the forces of his deepest desires. And his overwhelming love for her had given him the freedom to let go during lovemaking . . . to release the feelings deep within his heart and soul, as well as to satisfy the needs of his body.

Even with Amber . . .

But Sam clamped ruthlessly down on that thought. He would never make comparisons between the only two women he had ever loved.

But Lord, he had never thought this was possible! Never before had he been able to let go of his inhibitions. Until Eve, he had always held himself in check.

Maybe it was because he had been able to open to her this afternoon about the pain of his childhood. Maybe it was because she had trusted him enough to reveal some of her own hurts. Whatever the reason,

Sam now knew that he could let his passions have full reign and not hurt the woman he loved.

Only when long seconds went by and Eve didn't say a word, did Sam realize something was very wrong. A chill of apprehension ran up his back.

"Eve? Darling, what's the matter?. Oh, dammit, you're crying. I was too rough with you, wasn't I?"

"No. Oh, no, Sam . . . you were wonderful. Everything you did was absolutely perfect," she assured him, only to have her words choked off by a racking sob.

Sam rolled away from her to turn on the bedside light. By the time he returned to gather her into his arms again, Eve had stopped crying and now seemed to be hiccuping . . . or giggling . . . or both.

"Eve," he roared. "Tell me this instant what's going on?"

She looked at him. One hand clamped itself over her mouth, as if to stem the tide of her laughter, while the other hand pointed to the rumpled sheets.

He looked to where she indicated. "Oh, Eve. I did hurt you! Or. . . Or. . . Dammit, why didn't you tell me? I would have been more careful. Somehow, I would have gone slower. Sweetheart, why didn't you let me know you were a virgin?"

"Why? Don't you see, darling Sam, it's because I didn't know . . . I didn't know I was a virgin, either."

And with that statement, Eve went off on another round of hiccuping giggles.

Chapter Eleven

Sam pulled the top sheet from the bed and wrapped it around Eve's shaking body. She started to protest, but he had already gathered her up into his arms.

"We're going to take us a nice, soothing bath," he said in explanation as he marched out of the room and into the mirrored dressing area on the way to the bathroom's huge tub.

As bewildered as she was, Eve couldn't help noticing the dramatic, romantic picture they made in the parallel mirrors. There was Sam, tall and handsome and wonderfully nude, carrying his disheveled and slightly disoriented conquest from her boudoir to her bath. Their images bounced back and forth between the mirrors, to be reflected over and over in the glass. Over and over again? Over and over again!

"It's all in the mirrors, Sam!" Eve suddenly cried out. Her mind had done it! Everything had finally fallen into perfect order in her brain. She could even explain what had just happened during their lovemaking! "Stop, oh, please stop and look at the mirrors."

Sam halted his progress through the dressing room to drop a kiss on Eve's forehead. "Hush, sweetheart,

I'm only going to run a warm bath for you. It'll help with...uh, any soreness."

"I know, darling, and that will be wonderful...in a minute. But first look at the mirrors, Sam. Please put me down and look at us in the glass."

A frown of confusion furrowed Sam's wide brow, nevertheless he did what Eve begged of him. Carefully letting her down, he held her at his side while examining the mirror in front of him. He saw a copy of himself in it, and another in the mirror behind him.

All at once, standing between the parallel reflectors, Sam felt as if he were in a fun house. His image, multiplied by the arrangement of the glass, seemed to curve away into infinity.

"This is our reality, Sam." Eve's voice vibrated with excitement. "Look! There are a dozen Eves and a dozen Sams reflected back and forth in the mirrors. But, in fact, if there were enough light, we would see *infinite* numbers of us in there. That's what just dawned on me. Do you understand, darling? This is what the real cosmos is actually like."

"Honey...these are only our reflections that are being multiplied by the mirrors, not us. You're sounding like someone in a 'Star Trek' episode."

"Ms. Spock, you mean?" Eve awarded Sam with a kiss on the cheek when he turned red and began to sputter. "Admit it, dear, that was your very thought, wasn't it?"

"Well... I have heard the nickname, but I've always admired Spock—"

"You just don't want to date a Vulcan?" Eve laughed. "Well, too late...you're stuck with me. And I'm going to finish telling you this, even if I do sound like Spock, or Data...or—"

"Okay, okay," Sam broke in. "I give up. Please, be my guest and continue."

"I always intended to," Eve said with a saucy grin. But then she looked at the mirrors again, and her face became serious. "Sam, I wasn't talking about these *reflections* in the mirrors. What we're seeing here is only an analog. It's a model that shows us how the time-space continuum really works. There are an infinite number of universes in the cosmos, peopled by an infinite number of Sams and Eves. I've read serious scientific papers and mathematical proofs to back me up."

Sam was shaking his head, and Eve somehow knew that the gesture was not so much to counter what she was trying to explain, as it was an expression of his frustration. He wanted to get her into that tub in the next room, where warm water could ease the tension knotting the muscles in her shoulders and soothe tender, torn tissues.

But now that she knew just what had happened to her, and what was going to happen tomorrow, Eve had to make him understand it, too. With that in mind, she sank down on the rug between the mirrors and tugged at Sam's hand. After a second's hesitation, he followed her, wrapping his long arms around one raised knee.

Somehow, she managed to ignore the image he made, looking like a classic Greek sculpture that had come to warm, vibrant life. She had to ignore the lure of his naked body, because time was running out.

A clock had just appeared in her mind. Its second hand moved relentlessly toward the destructive release of geologic forces nobody could stop. But with Sam's help, perhaps they could lessen the extent of the human suffering that would follow the cataclysmic event.

"Eve, I don't understand..." Sam's concerned voice refocused her attention on him. Lines of worry creased his wide forehead. "What do you—"

"No, darling." She held up a staying hand. "Just listen to me first, and then ask all the questions you want."

When he nodded, she went on with her revelation. "Sam, there's a widely accepted theory that every time we make a choice, there's a split in the fabric of time and space. Look, I'm raising my right hand...but I just as easily could have lifted the left one."

Eve put one arm up in the air, and then the other. "And each time it happens...with each choice we make, a new universe splits off from the original one. At first, the two are identical, except for the consequences of that initial decision. But then, with every new choice that's made, each world diverges more and more.

"The more important the choice, the bigger the differences become, until the effects would be noticeable to someone who visited both of the universes. Someone like me."

"Okay, that's enough. Time out, Eve," Sam broke in.

Eve felt the urgent need to go on, but it was obvious Sam needed to digest this much before she explained the rest to him.

"I know the theory you're talking about, Eve. Alternate universes. The Sarban book you let me borrow yesterday describes what life might be like if Germany had won World War II. And there were half a dozen novels using the parallel world theme on your bookshelf at home. Don't you think, subconsciously, that's where you got this idea?''

"Sam...I hear what you're saying, but this—" she indicated their multiple images in the mirrors "—this answers everything. Don't you see? I am *not* the Eve you were introduced to a month ago. And you're not the same Sam I met, either. We haven't known each other four weeks, darling. We first laid eyes on each other yesterday, when I regained consciousness in the corridor behind the research labs."

"Eve! Eve, that's another thing. You had a bad fall yesterday and—"

"No! No, you can't blame this on that bump to my head, Sam. Everything fits too well. First of all, I am not concussed or crazy...and I do not have amnesia. In fact, I haven't lost the last month, or *any* of my memory. What really happened is that on New Year's Eve, in my own world, I was somehow thrown back in time—about two and a half days—and into another universe. I fell into the life of this universe's Eve Gray. I'm in a world parallel to my own. Your world, Sam.''

"NOW, JUST LAY BACK and soak for a few minutes. Is the water too hot?''

"No, it's fine, Sam. The tub is wonderful, the bubbles are wonderful, and so are you," Eve pronounced, scooping up a handful of the scented froth and leaning forward to decorate his chin with the lather.

Sam just grinned and settled back in the tub, his long legs stretched out on either side of her body. The water level rose to cover his chest...the vast expanse smooth and unadorned by hair.

Thank goodness for the bubbles, Eve thought. Because without them covering Sam's most notable charms, she knew it would be impossible to keep her mind on the subject at hand—convincing Sam she really had been thrown back in time and into another universe.

Her last statement in the dressing room had been one too many for him. He had picked her up and declared they both desperately needed to take a warm, calming bath.

Unsaid was the thought Eve could almost see running in bold letters across his forehead: that while he loved her dearly, Eve Gray was a space case!

"Now that we're all comfortable, are you ready to listen to this again, Sam?"

"Oh, Eve, did anybody ever tell you that you're one stubborn woman?" Wiping some foam from his face, Sam threatened to throw it at her. But then he chuckled instead and nodded his head. "All right, little mule, go on . . . tell it to me again, from the top."

"From the top?" she murmured, ignoring the gentle dig and resting her head against the tiled wall behind the tub. "Well, I guess it's best to start with the first time I saw you."

"On December 1st, in your office when Julie introduced us."

"No, in my universe, it was the night before that, November 30th. I had worked late and needed to get some things from the grocery store. I pulled into the Safeway parking lot, singing that horrible jingle from Mozart's fortieth symphony at the top of my lungs, and there you were. You were sitting in the next car—a late-model dark blue station wagon—listening to me bellow, with a big grin on your face. Little did you know you had become infected."

"Infected? Eve, I don't remember any of this. I've never driven a station wagon in my life, and what do you mean, horrible jingle? How could you singing some theme from the fortieth infect me with anything?"

"Sam, that's right! All of that happened in my *old* universe. Terrific! It means I didn't contaminate *you* . . . the Sam of this world. Oh, this is getting so confusing. Sam, let's keep everything in my perspective and call the guy from my original universe Sam One. And the Eve from your universe, my counterpart, will be Eve Two. I guess you didn't meet *her* until December 1st."

"Eve . . ."

"No, just listen until I'm finished, and then you can cart me off to the booby hatch," Eve said, giddy with the knowledge that she was absolutely sane.

"Okay, go on. I'll listen until the water cools."

"Then I'll make it fast. Starting again . . . in my original universe, I saw you—or rather, Sam One—for the first time in the Safeway parking lot on November 30th. I thought he was kind of cute, but I resisted making a fool of myself by trying to pick him up inside the grocery store."

"I wouldn't have minded getting propositioned by you, Eve," Sam said with a leer that looked even more silly because a few bubbles still clung to his chin.

"But remember, it wasn't *you* you in that store, Sam. It was Sam One. Oh, would you just let me get on with this?"

Sam wiped the grin and the remaining foam off his face with a wet hand, and then indicated that Eve should continue.

"Well, even though I didn't approach Sam One in the store, the flying fickle finger of fate wasn't going to let me get away with that choice. Julie formally introduced me to him the next morning, on December 1st. That's when I learned he was married. Or at least that he had on a wedding band."

Sam looked down at his hand and murmured, "I took my ring off the day I buried Amber. It's in a safe-deposit box."

"Sam, I know some of this is going to be painful for you . . . but . . ."

"No, go ahead, Eve, I guess I have to hear the rest of it."

"Well, we worked together, Sam One and I, for the month of December. Julie and Tawny and Hertha tried hard to find out something about that Sam's wife, but all they came up with was her name . . . Amber. The Monterey Yentas were so excited when they learned she was coming to the New Year's Eve party at the facility. By the way, that celebration is going to happen again tomorrow night, Sam. Just before they test the new communication device."

"But, Eve, you told me at Lovers' Point that you had memories of a devastating quake occurring on the Hayward Fault, just before the LinkUp test."

"Yes, Sam. And there will be an earthquake there tomorrow night, as well. The geology of the area hasn't changed. It's got to be the same in all of the parallel universes anywhere near my own. The forces involved in earthquakes are millions of years in the making and have little to do with the choices we make during our insignificant life spans Except for those decisions that occur if we happen to get caught in one."

"But . . . but . . ."

"Sam, you promised to just listen." Eve tried to calm her rising sense of panic. Unless she could get Sam to believe her, she would have to act on her own . . . and quickly.

"I'll try to be quiet," he mumbled.

"Good. Where was I? Oh . . . meeting Amber. I didn't want to meet her. Yet I had to. Sam, I was crazy about you . . . I mean, your counterpart, and I was so unhappy. I hated the idea of infidelity, and thank God, you—he—only treated me as a friend. All we ever did together was talk over coffee in the cafeteria. But I finally decided that I had to go to the party to meet Amber, with the hope that if I got to know her, I would be able to stop desiring him."

"So what happened then between you and this Sam One guy?" Sam muttered, as if he resented being caught up by her story.

Or perhaps, Eve thought, trying to suppress a happy grin, perhaps this Sam resented the thought of her wanting another man . . . even another version on himself.

"Well, I think my meeting Amber worked," she said, having conquered the urge to laugh. "I think I came to terms with the impossibility of the situation. But I'll never know now."

"I don't understand. Now that's an understatement! But why will you never know?"

"Because the earthquake happened at exactly five minutes after eleven. I never saw Amber and Sam One again."

"Did they die? Was Amber injured, Eve? Listen to me, I'm talking like I believe this is possible." Sam smacked his forehead with his palm.

"Sam...no, they didn't die, and neither of them was hurt. Nobody was injured at the facility. In fact, about an hour later they decided to go on with the LinkUp test according to schedule."

"Then what did you do?"

"Well, right after the eleven o'clock quake, I went into the communications room. I watched the monitors in there as all the terrible damage reports began to trickle in. Hertha and Joe were with me. They were worried about their family up in San Francisco. Hertha's daughter just had given birth. Just like here, in this universe.

"Anyway, I was worried about my sister, even though we hadn't spoken for a year. I hoped I could use the equipment to contact her, but they wouldn't let anyone make personal calls. It was close to midnight when I decided to get my purse and shawl out of my desk drawer and go home."

"So you kept valuables there in your original universe, too?" He grinned mischievously.

Eve's hopes that Sam was beginning to believe her soared, until she saw the twinkle in his eyes and understood that he was only teasing. He still didn't believe a word of what she had been saying. Sighing, she continued.

"Yeah...bad habits seem to span the cosmos. Anyway, I was on my way to my office when the aftershock happened. It must have been about midnight. I fell, hit my head, and when I awoke I was in your arms. And everything was different."

"Everything?"

"Well, no... actually, most things—like the whole complex—were the same. Only it was day instead of night... and December 29th, instead of New Year's Eve. But, at first, I didn't even know the date. I reasoned that I had been suffering from amnesia for some time and it must be early January. That explanation seemed to work... for a little while."

"But then..." Sam raised an eyebrow.

"Then you took me home. Remember?" Eve waited for Sam to nod before continuing. "I was still dazed when I went in to take that nap, but when I woke up, I started noticing how different everything was, compared to the reality that was stored in my memory."

"I don't understand."

"The placement of the furniture. Do you recall how I kept bumping into everything? And the Christmas tree! Sam... I didn't put one up this year, not in my universe, anyway. And you... you were so different from the Sam I had known for a month. You... you came on to me! You kissed me, touched me. And he, Sam One, had always treated me like a friend—no more, no less."

"And that would scare you. I do remember how uptight and angry you were every time I tried to get near you."

"Sam, I thought you were married! In my memory, I had just met your wonderful wife for the first time and I liked her so very, very much."

"My wife? Amber..." Sam turned his head to the tiled wall, but not before Eve saw his face pale. Here

was her opportunity to prove to Sam she was telling
the truth. Yet, it would hurt him so much to find out
that his wife lived—lived somewhere else—in a place
where he could never go. Eve felt tears well in her eyes,
but she knew she had to go through with it.

"Yes, Sam, I have met Amber. Listen to me, Sam.
Amber is tall . . . a little taller than I am. She's got carrot-red hair, blue eyes and is very, very thin . . ."

"No! Wrong, Eve." Sam's narrowed eyes snapped
back to her face. They were filled with anger—and
disgust. "And here I was, halfway up the road to be-
lieving you. Pretty good guessing, but you only got
three out of four. A redhead, with blue eyes . . . right.
And tall. Yes, she was taller than you. But she had
never been thin in her entire life. She was definitely
what they call pleasingly plump. While we were engaged, Amber went on a diet every Monday, and fell
off it by Wednesday, until I told her that I loved her
just as she was. I explained to her that I liked a woman
with a healthy appetite and plenty of flesh on her
bones! Just like you, Eve."

Sam suddenly got up. A wash of water threatened
to swamp over the edge of the tub with his exit. He
grabbed the His and Hers bathrobes hanging on the
back of the door. After shrugging into the larger one,
he held out the other for Eve.

"Time's up. The water's freezing. Here, come on
out and put this on."

When she hesitantly stood up, Sam flipped open the
drain, then, grabbing Eve's hand, helped her out.
Wrapping her in the robe, Sam took her elbow and
guided her back through the dressing area. He stopped
for a few seconds, looking at their multiple images,

before continuing into the bedroom. Back in there, he sat Eve on the bed.

Without a word, he threw himself down next to her, flinging his arm over his eyes.

Eve knew how much he had to be hurting, but she couldn't stop now. She would never forgive herself if she gave up.

"Sam, I don't understand about...about Amber being...plump. But I was right about the rest. I also recall she wore several rings and bracelets she had made herself. She was a jewelry designer. In fact, do you remember the ring you saw on the street vendor's stand this afternoon? I'm sure it was one of hers...and you...you seemed to think so, too. Didn't you, Sam?"

He shook his head, but in confusion rather than denial.

"Sam, I can also tell you about your own ring," she plowed on. "I know Amber made your wedding rings. Here, let me see if..."

Eve pulled open the bedside table drawer, looking for paper. She found some stationery and a pen, then quickly sketched the design of the wedding bands.

"I'm certainly not an artist, but this is more or less what I remember—shells made from gold, interlocked in a circle. Each shell is of a different species found near her home in Australia."

"Australia! How did you know about Australia? I know I never told Julie that Amber was from there."

"Sam...that's right! I forgot to tell you the most important thing I recall about Amber. You met her in Perth, where she was going to school. The Uni, she called it. But she came from somewhere farther north...some islands. Although, she wasn't born there, either. Amber told us at the party she originally lived on a sheep ranch, a station. But her mother divorced her father and remarried a lobster fisherman..."

Eve stopped talking to focus the scene in her mind. Like a tape, she rewound it, and then played back Amber's exact words.

"Abrolhos...Abrolhos Islands. That's it! She lived in the Abrolhos Islands before she went away to school."

Sam jerked upright and stared at Eve, his eyes as dangerous as dark blue lasers.

"I knew Julie was inquisitive, but I never thought she would use her position to break into my personal records. She must have gotten access to Amber's immigration papers to find out this sort of detail. Did you and Tawny help her get around the computer security codes, Eve?"

"Sam! How can you say such a thing? That's not true, any of it. Julie and Tawny are too ethical, and I'm—"

"Eve, do you really expect me to believe this cockamamy story about alternate universes, instead?"

"Yes, I do, Sam. Yes, I hoped that's just what you would do. Tell me, why would I go to such lengths to make up a story like this? What motive would I have...what would I gain? Well, I can see from your high opinion of my morals that I've been wasting my time. And that's the one thing I can't afford to do right now."

Eve grabbed up her clothes and ran for the bathroom. Slamming the door and locking it behind her, she quickly dressed.

When she came out again, Sam had also put on his shirt and pants, and was waiting for her in the dressing area.

"Eve, what do you think you're doing? Where are you going?" he demanded when she pushed by him and stalked into the living room.

Picking up her purse from the coffee table, she whirled on him. "I'm going to the nearest police or fire station to tell them there's going to be a major earthquake here tomorrow night, and they'd better get ready. That's where I'm going."

"Eve, they won't listen to you. You'll be arrested, or sent to..."

"To the funny farm? Just like *you* think I should be?"

"No...I don't. It's just so hard..." He sank down onto one of the suite's overstuffed chairs and put his head into his hands.

Suddenly feeling all the anger drain from her body, Eve dropped her purse and went to him. Sitting on the edge of the seat cushion, she put her arms around his shoulders and turned his head toward her breast. His hands buried themselves in her hair, his fingers stroking its thickness as if the repetitive motions were somehow soothing for him.

"I'm so sorry, Sam. So sorry," Eve crooned into his ear. "I know how hard it must have been to listen to me talk about Amber. But it was the only way I could think of to get you to believe me. I had to tell you things about her that I couldn't have known, except after meeting her.

"Things I couldn't have known!" As she repeated the phrase, Eve felt hope surge in her once again.

"Sam, listen, there's more. Tell me, did Amber ever make a pavlova for you?"

He raised his head, and looked at the expectant light shining from Eve's eyes. Slowly he nodded.

"And she used kiwi fruit on it, because she was deathly allergic to strawberries . . . didn't she?"

"Eve . . . How . . . how could you know that?"

"Yes, how could I know that? It's not the kind of thing that's required on immigration reports, is it? Julie—even if she had done what you thought— couldn't have found out that sort of information, could she?"

"I guess not . . . Although, I don't remember just what the medical portion might have asked. But . . ."

"And, Sam, I remember something else. She had a nickname for you, didn't she? There was a love code word that only the two of you shared, wasn't there?"

"Eve . . ." He stopped, and then opened his mouth. "Yes, it was . . ."

"No, don't tell me! I'll tell you. Boomer. It was Boomer, wasn't it?"

"God in heaven, how did you know that? It was just between the two of us. She only used it when . . ."

"I don't think I want to hear any more," Eve said, hastily holding up her hand to stop the revelation. Some things were sacred, after all. "But I knew about it because it slipped out when she was talking to you at the party. You turned—or should I say, your counterpart turned—the prettiest shade of pink when she said it."

"I can imagine," Sam said, his skin about the same tone as Eve had just described. "Eve, how could this have happened? How could you have traveled between parallel universes?"

Eve closed her eyes for a second. Did he believe?

"Does that mean you finally accept what I've told you, Sam?" Eve hopped off the chair and stood directly in front of Sam, her hands akimbo.

"Yeah...I guess I really do. At least until I can think of a better theory." He laughed at the indignant glare she arrowed at him. Tugging on her hand, he pulled her fully onto his lap and gave her an uncomplicated, affectionate hug.

Eve responded with a light kiss on his cute, snub nose, and a ruffle of slender fingers through his thick, dark hair.

"But, Eve, how do you think this happened?" he asked again, obviously needing to get all his mental ducks in a row.

"I'm not sure, Sam. Something about the earthquake...the aftershock, anyway. I don't really know."

"And there's something else I don't understand," Sam said. "Eve, if you and Lange were engaged...both here and in the other timeline, why..."

"Why was I still...untried...here, and not there? Well, I guess because it wasn't my body that got transported into the past, and into this universe. Only my mind, my memories—my soul, if you like—was sent here. This is Eve Two's body, not mine. And it seems she was a lot smarter than I was about Steven.

"She must have listened to her roommates' warnings, at least enough so she didn't feel ready to commit her body to him. I don't know... Oh, Lord, Sam...I just realized that I also have no idea what happened to *my* body in my original universe.

"Did it become a vegetable? Or did yet another Eve's mind pop into it? And what happened to the mind of the Eve who was here...the Eve you knew?

Do you realize she was the woman you really pursued for a month?'' And loved?

''You fell in love with him! That other Sam, not me,'' the man of this universe protested.

''Oh, Sam . . . I was just going to say you fell in love with her . . . Eve Two. And I guess it should matter exactly which one of us it was that attracted us in the first place. But can you honestly say it does? Do you feel any differently about the Eve you met yesterday, than you did about the woman you'd known for a month?''

He looked at her for a long minute. ''No . . . Yes! Yes, I do, Eve. I feel even more for you—the *you* I've been with these past two days. In fact, when I held you in my arms while you regained consciousness in the corridor, I found I couldn't control my feelings for you any longer. I had to touch you, to kiss you.''

''Oh, Sam, and I had to return that kiss. I couldn't help myself, either. And I felt so guilty.''

''Well, there shouldn't be any guilt, anymore. We have each other now. And you've said that in your original world, Amber has Sam One. Eve, I can't tell you what a gift you've given me, dearest heart. To think that somewhere, somehow, Amber is alive and well, and happy. She was happy, wasn't she, Eve?''

''Oh, yes,'' Eve said without hesitation. ''I've never seen two people who were happier with each other.''

She didn't add she had just figured out the weight difference between the Amber she had met and the woman who had been this Sam's wife.

Now that she had a chance to think about it, at least subconsciously, it was so clear. The Amber of Eve's original universe had been terribly injured in the car crash. She had been through a number of operations to restore her ability to walk. Of course, she would be bone thin. If not from the procedures, than as an imperative from her doctors to keep excess weight off, so her bones and muscles could heal as quickly as possible.

But that was something Eve would never tell Sam. It would be too cruel to tell him that, while not dead, Amber had suffered for years from the aftereffects of the accident.

"So, it seems we're all dressed up with nowhere to go," Sam said while tugging on the hem of Eve's sweater.

"Stop, Sam." Eve held on to his hands. "We have lots of places to go. But I'm not sure where to start."

"Start?"

"Sam, there's going to be a horrible earthquake in—" she checked her watch "—in just under twenty-four hours. We have to warn people, to alert the authorities. And I have to find my sister, to tell her what's going to happen."

"Eve, sweetheart—it's not going to be that easy."

"Oh, I know, Sam. We don't want to create a panic. That would probably cause more death and injury than the quake itself. But the emergency people must have a plan to evacuate key areas in an orderly manner."

"I'm sure they do, Eve, if they believe us."

"Believe us? But, Sam—I told you, and you finally believed me, didn't you?"

"Yes. Yes, I did—I do. But only because you convinced me with things you couldn't have possibly known without having met Amber. Do you really think the fact my wife was allergic to strawberries, or had a private pet name for me is going to cut the mustard with the mayor, or the emergency people?"

"Well...no... I see what you mean. Oh, Sam, what can we do?"

"We've got to get to someone who can make an earthquake prediction based on a solid reputation. Someone with impeccable credentials. And I know just the guy to call, my roommate from college, Dave Sutter."

Sam scooted Eve off his lap and after plopping her back down on the chair, strode over to the phone. He spent a minute riffling through the city directory. Punching up a number he found there, his long fingers drummed the table while he waited.

"Dave. Were you asleep? Sorry, old man. Sam...it's Sam Davidson. Yeah, it's been too long. We *should* get together soon. What about in half an hour?"

Suddenly too nervous to remain seated, Eve got up and paced while she listened to Sam's end of the conversation.

"No, I'm in Berkeley right now. At the Maritime Hotel. Look, Dave, I'm not kidding. I have something very serious I want to discuss with you... something I need the best geologist in the state to listen to. No, I think it would be better to meet you at your lab, or wherever it is that you can tie into your prediction computer. You have a setup at your house? Great! The directory says you're at 5555 South Oak. Okay, we'll be there soon. Yeah, you can say I'm bringing a friend...my fiancée, except she doesn't know that's what she is, yet. See you."

Sam hung up the phone and then shrugged into his suit jacket.

"Sam?" Eve found she couldn't say anything more than his name. Had he really just proposed?

"We'll have to talk about our future a bit later, sweetheart," Sam said, running his fingers down her arm, then taking her hand. "Come on, let's get going. David is the best geologist around. If anybody can get the authorities to listen to a prediction, it will be him. All we have to decide on the way over is just what to tell him."

"Wouldn't the truth be best, Sam?"

"Maybe. Or maybe we should tell him something more believable...like you're an incredibly talented psychic!"

Chapter Twelve

"I'm sorry, Sam...Eve, there just isn't anything definite here. And I can't issue a prediction without something concrete to back me up. Nobody would listen."

David Sutter ran his fingers through his prematurely gray hair. Turning away from the computer screen, where he had been accessing the latest data from the U.S. Geologic Survey on area earth movements, Dave looked up at the two people hovering over his shoulder.

His unusual hazel eyes were filled with sincere regret.

"But, Dave, what about everything Eve told you? I know a lot of it sounds screwy, insane, off-the-wall..."

"Oh, I can do better than that, Sam," Eve broke in. "You're trying to tell Dave I'm more than a few bricks short of a full load...working on only three cylinders...my elevator doesn't go to the top floor...my picnic is a half-dozen sandwiches short...the cheese fell off my cracker a long time ago..."

Both men threw back their heads, laughing long and hard. Eve let out a ladylike snort and plopped down on a nearby couch. Still laughing, Sam came over and sat beside her. Putting an arm around her shoulders, he gave her a squeeze of apology.

"Eve, I'm sorry," Dave finally said when he recovered his breath. "You don't seem crazy to me. Just the opposite, in fact. You've presented a very compelling and logical theory to account for what's happened to you. Everything you've experienced could be explained by you having traveled between parallel universes. However, there's no documentation. You don't have any hard facts we can use to convince other scientists and the authorities."

Dave reached over and opened a storage box containing dozens of CD-ROM disks. He took one out and held it up.

"Let me spell out the problem for you. See this disk and the rest? You both know how much information can be stored on each of them . . . several encyclopedias' worth. And every one of these is filled with the legitimate data we've collected on earthquakes around the world. But it still is not enough for anyone to make a realistic prediction, even though scientists have been looking for some accurate way to give advanced warning of major earthquakes for decades.

"They've examined everything from animal runaways to water level changes, from increases in emissions of radon, to gravity fluctuations . . ."

Putting the disk back, Dave got up from his chair. He began pacing back and forth in front of them as he talked.

"And when there were strange increases in electromagnetic fields just before the Loma Prieta quake back in 1989, everyone jumped on that bandwagon as a promising area to research. But for all the studies, for all the experimental devices set up around known earthquake sites—like Parkside, near you in Monterey—no one has ever come up with a reliable way to predict a significant earthquake.

"In fact, our track record had been so miserable the government shut down the Parkside array in early 1995. They also cut back funding for some very promising experiments. And that wonderful group up in Washington even talked about eliminating the U.S. Geologic Survey!"

"I didn't realize things were so bad," Sam said.

"Well, they are. And probably are not going to get any botter. So, Eve, as much as I'd like to believe you have knowledge of a coming quake—hell, I'm more than halfway convinced myself that you do—I still have to think of the future of earthquake prediction. Because if I stick my neck out and I'm wrong, that's it for my research grants, and my credibility for the next hundred years. But more important, a false prediction on my part would taint all the other scientists who are working in the field."

"Well, I guess that's it," Sam said, rising from the couch, then giving Eve a hand up. "Sorry for waking you and keeping you going at this till two in the morning, Dave."

Sam stuck out his hand and gave his friend a quick goodbye shake. "We'll be at the Maritime until nine or so this morning, and then we hope to get back to Monterey by noon. Give us a call if you change your mind, or think of something else we can do."

"Sam... Dammit, let me give you a few numbers of people who might be of some help. Although, what you can say to them that won't sound.... Hell, forget that. Let me talk to them myself and call in a few chips owed to me. At the very least, I should be able to get an unofficial upgrading to a higher alert status. It will mean some more fire and police people on duty, and hospital staff put on call...that sort of thing. Of course, what we really need is for them to get everybody out of nonductile concrete-frame buildings, and shut down the freeways. But nobody's going to do that with the kind of information we've got."

"Thank you, Dave. Hopefully, the extra manpower will make some difference. You've made me feel a bit better," Eve said, giving him a quick hug.

They were outside the front door when Sam turned back to his friend. "I forgot to ask, Dave...are you working on any particular theory yourself?"

"Oh, I've been concentrating on measuring fluctuations in the earth's magnetic field."

"And have you noticed anything unusual around here in your readings for the last few days?"

David Sutter looked at Sam and then Eve. He grimaced, and then shrugged his shoulders. "There may be *something* happening around the Hayward Fault that's statistically significant. But I can't be sure until..."

"Until the quake happens at five after eleven tonight," Sam finished for him.

It was almost three in the morning when Eve and Sam climbed naked into the huge bed in their hotel suite. He gathered her into his arms, to share with her a deep, soul-satisfying kiss. Then with a heartfelt sigh, he spooned his big, warm body around hers and granted them what they both needed most...a few hours' sleep.

Eve woke with a smile, and a plan. The smile was for the gorgeous man sprawled next to her on the bed, and the plan was a brilliant strategy of how she was going to get her sister out of the city before the earthquake hit.

Creeping into the other room just before eight, she searched her purse for the card Steven had given her the night before. Taking a chance someone might be in early, Eve dialed Janet's lawyer.

"Cohan and Cohn," a feminine voice answered on the third ring.

"Uh...are you real, or is this your voice mail thingie?"

"I'm as real as anyone can be at 8:00 a.m. on the last day of the year."

"Oh, good. This is Eve Gray. I left a message on your recorder last night. I'd like to talk to Susan Cohn about my sister, Janet Lange."

"I hadn't checked messages yet. What is this in regards to?" the voice asked, all business now.

"It's a request. Nothing to do with my sister's...divorce," she assured the woman. "Will Ms. Cohn be in soon?"

"This is she speaking...I have an early court date and needed some paperwork. Can you be more specific about the nature of the request?"

"Well, it's a bit strange, but a handsome reward is involved." Eve crossed her fingers behind her back, hoping Janet would agree with her about that. She had heard the desperation in Steven's voice last night, and had to admit that he did love her sister. He loved Janet, and perhaps the shock of her leaving had finally made him grow up.

"You see, a friend wants Janet to do a portrait of himself, as a surprise for his wife," Eve continued explaining to the lawyer. "But there are a couple of conditions."

"Which are?"

"Janet has to be in Lake Tahoe by ten this evening, and work throughout the night on the...commission."

"And can you vouch for this man?"

"Oh, yes," Eve assured her. And if Steve disappointed Janet this time, Eve would personally break every one of his beautifully capped teeth. "There will be a reservation made for her at the Thunderbird Lodge, at his cost. And he will also have everything she needs to work on the project."

"All right, as you said, this is a bit strange. But I'll try to pass the information on to your sister. Have a good day."

"Thank you. The same to you. Uh, do you have any special plans for celebrating the New Year tonight?" Eve couldn't help asking.

"Yes. I'm leaving with my family for a vacation right after I get out of court."

"Terrific! I mean, have a good time. Thank you."

Eve hung up before she could screw up by saying something really stupid.

She quickly dialed two more numbers. One was to make reservations at the Lake Tahoe lodge, the other was to her brother-in-law. Quickly outlining her plan, Eve then read him the riot act...telling him in graphic detail what fate he would suffer if he gave her sister another day's worry.

Hanging up with a smile of satisfaction on her face, Eve whirled around at the sound of soft laughter.

"Oh, Eve. I'm so glad you're on my side. And as I've said before...you have got a good heart."

"It belongs only to you, Sam." She went into his open arms and got the best good-morning kiss in this or any other universe.

"WELL, LET'S GO OVER our game plan again," Eve suggested as they neared the outskirts of Monterey just before noon.

"Sure. First, I'll stop off at my apartment and change clothes," Sam began. "Then we swing by your house. After that, I'll make calls to some of my own government contacts to see if they'll help upgrade that alert David talked about. I have their numbers at the facility. By the way, I'll also tell Julie that you're taking another day off, so you can go to your doctor's appointment . . . Say, wasn't that appoint—"

"Oh, I canceled it while you were showering back in Berkeley. There's nothing wrong with my head. Remember, we figured out why my memory seemed screwed up."

"Right, but you still should . . ."

"Get some sleep?" Eve broke in, starting her own mind-reading act with Sam. "Well, I'd rather help you with those calls, if I can. And as mundane as it seems in light of all that's happened—and *will* happen—the decorating committee still has to set up the cafeteria for the party tonight. We have to get ready for *another* New Year's Eve," she said with a wry smile.

SAM'S ONE-BEDROOM apartment was tiny. The main room was a combined living and dining area, with a counter and kitchen appliances set off at one end.

"It's a dump," Sam said cheerfully when he ushered Eve inside. "Wasn't expecting company, so watch where you walk. I'll just change . . . be back in five."

After Sam went through the open bedroom door, Eve watched with rapt attention while he quickly stripped off his rumpled suit and shirt. The casual intimacy of seeing him rummage around in his dresser for clean clothing, wearing only a cute pair of boxer shorts sparked hot tears in her eyes.

This was not a fantasy...Sam was really hers! Hers to love and hold close for the rest of her life.

He opened a closet door and extracted a dark gray suit. "Oh, Sam...remember, today is casual," Eve called into the room.

"Thanks...wish we could wear jeans all the time," he replied, putting back the suit and retrieving a faded denim shirt and Levi's jeans. Throwing the clothes on the bed, he went into a door Eve figured was the adjacent bathroom. The sound of running water confirmed her guess a few seconds later.

Released from his overwhelming presence, she wandered around the room. No practiced seducer of women lived here, she soon decided, with a secret sigh of relief that her judgment had been correct.

His decorating scheme consisted of one battered corduroy couch—with an attached end table and lamp arrangement—a huge stereo setup, and a computer work station.

Books were strewn everywhere. Eve noticed her copy of *The Sound of His Horn* on the end table. The envelope he had stuck inside as a bookmark indicated he was almost done with it.

Just then, she remembered the small bag she had in her purse. Reaching inside, she extracted the duplicate of the Sarban work she had bought for Sam in Berkeley. With an imp of a smile, she got out a pen, and quickly wrote a message on the inside of the front cover. She tiptoed into the bedroom and placed the novel on top of his fresh clothing.

Out in the living room once again, Eve sat down on the lumpy couch. She reopened the bag and took out the other Sarban book. She couldn't resist reading for a few minutes while Sam washed up.

Reaching over to turn on the end table light, her hand knocked a large picture frame. Placing it back upright, her fingers froze on the wood when she saw the face that smiled out at her.

Dimples, carrot-red hair, large blue eyes...Amber.

Yet, *not* Amber. For this young girl—she looked too fresh and innocent to be called a woman—had never known the pain the Amber of Eve's home world had experienced. And Sam was right, no one would have ever called her thin. Her cheeks were round and jolly, her chin had a little companion that attested to someone who loved good food and lots of it.

"Eve...Eve. Thank you, sweetheart," Sam's voice sounded from the next room.

Guiltily returning the picture to its place, Eve got up and walked to the bedroom door.

"I'll treasure it, always. And especially your words." Sam came over, shirt still unbuttoned on that magnificent chest. He bent and brushed his lips back and forth against Eve's willing mouth.

With a groan, she wrapped her arms around his naked waist and burrowed her nose into the junction where strong neck met wide shoulder. The clean, male scent of him overwhelmed her. She had never been so happy. It seemed almost a crime when she knew the devastation so many people would suffer tonight.

Maybe it was because her body suddenly stiffened at the disquieting thought, but Sam instantly moved back a step.

"We'll do what we can, Eve. But I'll not be ashamed of what I'm feeling right now. I've never loved anyone so much as you."

And in this moment, Eve had no doubts that he meant every word. He loved her more than *anyone*, and even if it made her seem petty and immature, she glowed with that knowledge.

"And you mean more to me than anyone, anywhere, Sam. As I said in the book, there is no other man for me in anytime, anyplace, any universe."

"Amen! Well, let's get over to your house," he said, grinning and buttoning his shirt.

"Sam, this is good enough for decorating the cafeteria. The wrinkles hung out a bit overnight." Eve gestured to her slacks and sweater.

"Okay. Then off we go to help save the world."

WHEN THEY ENTERED Sam's office, he immediately got on the phone and tried to contact anyone he thought might help mobilize the earthquake preparedness infrastructure.

Watching him go through the list of his contacts, Eve realized there really wasn't anything she could do here to help him. These people knew Sam...they would listen to him because of what they knew about him. They wouldn't have the vaguest idea who she was.

"Sam, I'm going over to the cafeteria," she finally said when he finished his conversation.

"Sounds good," he said, distracted and already punching the keys to connect with the next person.

Eve placed a quick kiss on his cheek and left the office.

"EVE, I'M SORRY this is so late. Joe and I just got back from seeing our new..."

"Don't say another word, Hertha." Eve put a finger on her friend's lips. "Wait just a minute with that news. Julie, would you come over here for a second?" Eve called across the cafeteria to where the redhead was putting together the decorations for one of the tables.

Hertha stood mute, looking at Eve as if wondering what had gotten into her, until Julie walked over to them.

"Julie, Hertha just arrived from San Francisco and was going to tell us about the birth of her third grandchild. Remember yesterday, when I predicted the baby would be a girl? Didn't I tell you that she would weigh nine pounds, seven ounces, and they would name her Melody Anne?"

"That's right, you did," Julie confirmed, head bobbing up and down. "Whoops, get Hertha into a chair!"

"Are you all right?" Eve asked after fetching a glass of cold water for the older woman.

"Yes...I think so. Eve, I didn't call anybody here with that information. And I know that Joe..."

"No, Joe didn't call me, either. Let's just say I've had a vision. But will you believe me when I say that I'm deadly serious about what I'm going to ask you to do next?"

Hertha looked into Eve's eyes and slowly nodded her head.

"All right. Hertha, I want you to phone your daughter and her husband, and have them get their children into their car and drive down to visit you. Right now!"

"Eve...she just got out of the hospital two days ago. The baby's less than a week old."

"Dear, I know. But believe me, I have a good reason for asking you to do this. Please call them. You'll be so happy you did."

Hertha looked into Eve's eyes again for several heartbeats. Whatever it was she saw there made her finally nod her head. "All right...all right. I'll go call her."

Eve gave her a hug of relief. She then took the banner Hertha had brought as her contribution to the party decorations over to Tom Lewis. The electrical engineer put up the sign, which had Happy New Year written in Portuguese, in a place of honor near the entryway.

Chapter Thirteen

It was almost six when Eve let herself into her house. She immediately walked to the phone and dialed Sam's home number. He had still been making calls in his office when she finished working on the decorations, but promised to leave in a few minutes.

After exchanging a passionate goodbye kiss in his office, they both agreed that Sam should go to his own apartment to sleep, or neither of them would get the rest they both desperately needed. Eve had driven home in her own car... which had been in the facility lot for two days.

"Sam, it's me," Eve said when he answered on the third ring. "How are you doing, darling?"

"Any time I hear you say 'darling' to me, darlin', I feel terrific. But as for the rest of it, well, I went up the chain of command at the California Office of Emergency Services and the Federal Emergency Management Agency. I finally got to talk to the top honchos from each organization after you left."

"And?"

"And they both think I've gone 'round the bend. They hinted about going to my superiors and asking them to evaluate my ability to head up computer security around here."

"Oh, Sam. I'm so sorry I've put you through all this. And now your career is in jeopardy and..."

"Eve...love. Not to worry. The worst thing that will happen is I'll lose this job. I'll just set up my own consulting firm, and marry you. Then, after you get your Ph.D. in mathematics, I'll help you raise our babies."

"So that's the worst?" Eve asked in a dazed whisper. "And what's the best?"

"I don't lose the job...and everything else is the same."

"Oh, Sam ... I love you so much."

"Not as much as I love you."

"Do, too!"

"Do not!"

"Is this our first argument, Sam."

"Nah, that'll come when we fight over what to name our first child. Eve, I'm going to crash for a couple hours, and then I'll be over to pick you up for the party."

"Do you think we should go? I think I'd rather stay here and work on making that first offspring of ours."

"You do pick your moments," Sam said with a husky chuckle. "But I have to be there when they fire up the test equipment. There's absolutely no doubt I'd lose my job if I miss that one."

"Okay, see you at nine, or so."

Eve hung up, a big smile on her face that only dimmed when she looked around the homey, yet alien, room.

Everything makes so much more sense now, she thought as she wandered around. Now she knew this

was her counterpart's home. It was so alike, yet sub-
tly different, from her own. She was sure when she had
time to make a careful comparison with the information stored in her mind, she would find a lot of things
missing here, and many new additions to the list.

Eve found herself wondering just when this particular universe had split off from her own timeline. Up
to what point were things identical, and what decisions had made them different?

Of course, Mozart had lived a few months longer in
this world. But it appeared that, except to musicolo-
gists, the additional works he had composed in that
period had made little difference to the subsequent
flow of historical events.

On a more personal level, Eve decided her world
had split into two timelines the instant she ignored her
roommates' warnings and gave herself to Steven for
the first time—just before her parents' deaths and Janet's appearance for their funeral.

But in this universe, Eve Two had not trusted Steven
enough to offer him that final commitment of body
and soul. *Smart cookie, Eve Two,* Eve One thought.

Yet, the end result had been almost the same—a
broken engagement, and the estrangement from her
sister. However, not having lost her virginity to Steven
in this universe, Eve Two must not have felt as dev-
astated as Eve had been. Her counterpart had been
able to face this year's holiday season with a lighter
heart.

Eve walked over to the alcove and switched on the
tree Eve Two had trimmed. As in past years, the soft,
pastel lighting sent a warm, inviting glow over her piano.

Pulling out the bench, she opened the lid protecting the keys and sat down. Eve couldn't remember the last time she had played just for herself, but fingers automatically found the proper position and a rich, full rendition of "Silent Night" poured forth from her memory.

Fighting back her tears, Eve played all the carols she and her family would have sung this year, if other decisions had been made.

In that perfect universe, her parents were still alive and she had not been betrayed by Janet and Steven. Of course, in that faultless parallel dimension, Eve would never have become involved with Steven in the first place, and Sam would have been her heart's first love.

Which meant Amber would be dead.

"Oh, Lord," she cried out loud, losing the battle with her tears. Letting go, she lamented her parents' needless deaths and she sorrowed that Amber's bright personality had been lost to this world. And Eve knew some of her tears were shed for the myriad versions of herself who lived in worlds where Sam's love was forever unattainable.

She mourned until all of her anguish, mistakes, and regrets were examined and then laid to rest.

When Sam arrived two hours later, Eve had slept a bit, then showered away all traces of her tears. She greeted him with a brilliantly happy smile and an enthusiastic hug.

"Wow, think I'll go away for another few hours, if you'll say hello like this again," Sam said, holding her at arm's length to admire her outfit. "Beautiful. A goddess in green."

"Glad you like it. Seems that your world's Eve went to the same Macy's department store sale as I did."

She laughed, hands smoothing down the fabric clinging to her hips.

With his face looking serious all of a sudden, Sam put his huge, tender hands on each side of Eve's face. "Are you ready for tonight, my love?"

"Yes . . . It's not going to be easy, is it, Sam?"

"No. Even if they go to a higher alert status, there will still be tremendous destruction of property, and a lot of deaths and injuries. Dammit, if only we had more time. If only Dave would have made that prediction."

"He did all he could . . . given the circumstances. I remember something Voltaire said. 'It is dangerous to be right in matters on which the established authorities are wrong.' Would you honestly have done more than he did, if someone came to you with our story?"

"Guess not. You're right, Eve. Let's go."

"Just let me give the Thunderbird Lodge a call to see if my sister and Steven got there."

Eve found the number and dialed. A minute later, she turned to Sam.

"They're not there, Sam. Neither one of them has checked in!"

SAM COULD FEEL the slight tremor in Eve's shoulders as they danced. Ten fifty-five. Ten minutes until the main quake hit. He had already done his duty by checking out computer security for the upcoming test at midnight. Theoretically, he wouldn't have to go back to the control room until almost twelve.

Eve couldn't tell him what would happen after the second quake. She had been transported at that instant into this world and back to the afternoon of December 29th.

"Do you want to sit down, sweetheart? Or do you want me to go get your shawl?" he asked when she continued to shiver.

"No, I just want your arms around me, and this is the only way we can do that right now," she said, moving even closer to him, pressing her hips against his and nestling her cheek into his neck.

Sam felt a surge of heat quicken his body where he and Eve were almost fused together. But unless he wanted to shock everybody around them, he couldn't move away from her right now, even if he wanted to.

His body had never been so out of control, not when he had been a randy teenager, not even with Amber. Around Eve, he was unable to dampen his lustful thoughts. She had the large breasts, tiny waist and generous hips any earth goddess would envy. And there was no man living who would be able to resist the pull of her innocent sensuality, or want to deny himself the thought of taking her lush body.

Sam abruptly found himself wondering about his counterpart in Eve's home universe. According to her, Sam One—as Eve called him—and Amber were still very much in love. But what about all the coffee breaks he and Eve had shared in that world's cafeteria?

Sam remembered the meetings here *he* had engineered, because he wanted to be with Eve. Somehow he doubted that his double's intentions were as innocent as she seemed to think they had been. What a moral battle that poor guy must have gone through.

He shied away from the thought of what would have happened if his Amber were alive and he suddenly had met Eve.

Well, it hadn't happened. Eve was here, and she was his! As if reading his thoughts, she snuggled even closer, causing further havoc with the parts of him that were already in serious trouble.

Sam tried to take his mind off his delightful dilemma by letting his gaze wander around the room. The first thing he noticed was Julie and Tawny. He had to grin at the looks on their faces.

They were obviously floored by the sight of Eve in his arms and willingly molding her body so close to his. With their heads bobbing up and down, the two ladies were whispering to each other, their mouths going a mile a minute.

Eve would be in for an intense grilling from those Monterey Yentas at the first opportunity. But that wouldn't be for several days, he knew. Everything would be in an uproar around here after the quake.

If it occurred.

Now where had that traitorous thought come from? *Admit it, Davidson. You still have your doubts.* If he really, truly, believed Eve, would he have given up so easily in trying to get an official prediction out of Dave?

Sam looked up at the big clock over the entry door. Five more minutes and he would know for sure, one way or the other. As if reading his thoughts, Eve's feet stopped moving. She looked up and examined his face.

"Maybe it would be safer if we sat down?" he asked, hoping he didn't look as guilty as he felt.

"No, no one gets knocked off their feet in here. But perhaps we should go over to the doorway, so we can get to the communications room as quickly as possible after the shaking stops. I want to see if there's any difference in the media reports."

"Okay, let's walk slowly over there," Sam agreed, trying not to feel as if he were just placating her. But if Eve was right and traveling between parallel universes really was possible, then they were walking toward the portal of a strange new universe, full of an infinity of possibilities.

And if Eve were wrong? Well ... hopefully there would not be any long-term effects from that blow to her head and she would be back to normal in a few days.

EVE STOPPED in the doorway and held on to Sam's hand. *How different it is this time,* she thought. She had ridden out the last quake on her own. Literally and figuratively, she'd had no one to hold on to in her own universe. Sam had been with Amber. Julie had been with her husband, Bob. And Hertha had Joe.

Hertha? Eve couldn't remember seeing the Jenkinses here tonight. She hoped that meant Hertha's daughter and her family were, even now, settling in at the Jenkinses home. She would call them in the morning and check.

"What time is it now?" Eve asked Sam, who immediately looked at his watch.

"Time, sweetheart ... it's just about— Oh, God!"

The floor jolted and rolled under their feet. Sam grabbed Eve tightly around the waist and pulled her into his body as he braced against the doorjamb. The shaking and vibrating seemed to go on forever, until it abruptly stopped.

"You all right?" Sam said. His face was pale.

"Yes. Are you?"

"It happened ... it really happened," he whispered, his eyes looking wildly around at the panic in the cafeteria for a second. "And that means everything else is true ... doesn't it, Eve?"

She simply nodded, not angry that he had still held on to some reservations about her story. She probably would have had the same lingering doubts if their positions had been reversed.

"Let's go listen to the reports, Sam," she said, tugging on his hand.

They were among the first people, other than the technicians, to get to the communications room. The banks of monitors were full of snow when they arrived. The links to the San Francisco area had obviously been cut this time, too. But Eve expected that. The big picture wouldn't have changed. The damage to structures would be the same. What she hoped and prayed was that their efforts had saved some lives.

"Where did it hit, and what was the magnitude?" someone in the growing crowd asked.

"Was it local?" another voice called out.

". . . indicate a strong earthquake hit the San Francisco area at five minutes after eleven, Pacific standard time. This is CNN," an announcer's voice boomed when one of the monitors came back on line.

"Stay tuned for more information as it's received. To repeat, all we know is that a strong earthquake has shaken the San—"

"Excuse me, folks, let me by." Eve turned to see Tom Lewis moving through the crowd.

"Tom, over here," Sam hailed him. "Any chance to use the equipment to contact people up north?" Eve knew he was referring to her sister.

"Sorry, the circuits are either out or overloaded. Hey, isn't it terrific! This is just the situation the LinkUp interface was designed for. . . rerouting telecommunications during a disaster. Hope they go through with the test. It could be used to get things back on line for everyone up north."

He indicated the reports scrolling down the screens on several monitors. Tom turned and headed for the scaffolding set against a wall. He climbed to the twelve-foot-high false ceiling. Pushing back a section of the plastic paneling, he crawled inside.

"He's got to check out the electrical cables up there for damage," Sam said in her ear.

Eve nodded, remembering the Tom from her original universe doing the same thing. She thought how strange it was that one man's disaster was another's opportunity. Turning her attention back to the monitors, she read the long series of reports that were coming in.

"All personnel. Attention, all facility personnel." A loudspeaker crackled to life overhead. "Preliminary reports just in indicate that a 7.1 earthquake, lasting approximately thirty seconds, has occurred on the Hayward Fault. The cities of Berkeley and Oakland are most affected. Reports of heavy road and building damage are coming in...the number of casualties has not been released..."

"Oh, Lord, I hope Janet and Steven left the city," Eve said, turning to Sam. He grabbed her hand and squeezed it hard.

"Eve, whatever happens, you did your best."

"But if I had only figured out what had happened to me, earlier, I could have had more time. Time enough to talk to Janet and Steven, to really explain. As it was, they would have thought I was crazy. That's why I set up that silly ruse..."

"Eve, don't blame yourself. Nobody could have done better. I used to think the way you are right now. For months, for a year, after Amber died, I would wake up at night in a cold sweat thinking, 'What if I had turned to the right, instead of the left? What if I had gone a little slower, or a little faster! What if..."'

"Yes...what if. And each what-if happened, didn't it, Sam? In some universes, there was no crash at all. In some universes, I got people to believe me...in others..."

"In others, we never got together, sweetheart. And for me, right now, that would have been the biggest tragedy of all."

Before Eve could voice her astonished reaction to Sam's fervent declaration, the CNN monitor blared an announcement.

"We now have a live feed from our reporter in the East Bay area of San Francisco," the commentator intoned. "John Jacobs has found a helicopter to fly him over the Berkeley area east of San Francisco. What you will see is live. We have no voice-over, so we'll try to interpret what is shown. Our experts say this quake will be much more destructive to the Bay area than the 1989 Loma Prieta 7.1 temblor, because the epicenter is so much closer."

There was a brief flicker and then a slightly out-of-focus, bobbing picture appeared.

"'That's a section of freeway fallen over on its side, cars strewn everywhere," the news anchor described. "And now we're over a block of buildings...smoke or dust is rising from the collapsed structures. You can see people wandering down this street. There's... Oh, no...a tilting building just gave way and fell—"

"Oh, Sam. This is just the same, it's happening just the same as last time. Those poor people. Sam...we didn't make any difference. All those calls you made didn't do any good. None of it did any good."

She went into his arms, and they stood for long minutes, watching the scenes unfold. They were still there half an hour later when the loudspeaker blared once more.

"All personnel involved with the linking experiment, go to your stations. There has been no damage to our equipment . . . phone lines are working here, so the test will go on as scheduled. Repeat, we are a Go for testing Project LinkUp. And if successful, we will stay on line and use the new interface to help reestablish worldwide communications with the San Francisco Bay area."

A cheer went up around the room. Eve watched as, one by one, the monitors shifted from earthquake coverage to rows of streaming numbers. The countdown clocks came alive. Five minutes till Project LinkUp.

Almost mesmerized, she watched the numbers run down.

"I should get to the computer room, sweetheart," Sam said.

"What? Oh, yes. Go on, Sam. Since the phone lines are working here, I think I'll walk over to my office and try to call Lake Tahoe again. I'll wait for you there."

Giving Sam a quick, hard kiss, Eve pushed out of the room. Walking as fast as her high heels would allow, she rushed through the corridors behind the testing labs. Somehow the countdown continued in her head.

Moving along the white-tiled hallway, she found herself chanting the numbers. "Ten, nine, eight . . ."

"Eve, Eve, wait . . . Don't go any farther. Come back here. I just figured it out . . ."

She whirled in the direction of Sam's voice and had a quick impression of him running toward her at full tilt . . . his hands outstretched for her.

"Oh, Lord! It's the second earthquake," she screamed even as the floor heaved and she felt her feet go out from under her body.

While she was falling—as if in slow motion toward the corner edge where the two corridors met—a deep rumbling vibration ran through every muscle in Eve's body. She felt the shuddering contact of one solid body hitting another, and then lights flared.

First red, then blue, followed by a swirling black dot that grew and grew until it swallowed up the wall, the corridor... and finally, Eve.

A word tore out of her throat in the last instant before her mind fell into that ebony whirlpool of unimaginable forces. One word. A shout, a name.

"Sam!"

"SAM!"

His name echoed in the tiled hallway. When Eve opened her eyes, she found that she was looking into a familiar pair of dark blue irises.

"Yes, it's me, Eve. It's okay. You're all right. I got to you before you hit the wall."

Eve's hand went to her head.

No blood...no bump...and no evidence of a healing cut.

Struggling into a sitting position, Eve looked into Sam's concerned dark blue eyes. A wave of fear surged through her in reaction to a sudden, horrible thought.

Grabbing Sam's left hand, she pulled it up in front of her face. A sigh slipped out of her throat.

"No ring," she whispered. He was not married. But was this her Sam, or yet another one?

"No... but there will be a ring on both our fingers in a day or two," Sam promised.

"Sam? Is it really you? Are you *my* Sam?"

"Yes, Eve...it's me, Sam Two. And you'll be stuck with this version for the rest of your life."

His mouth lowered to hers and the world spun away again.

"Ahem. Ahem! Mr. Davidson, Ms. Gray. Are you both all right?"

Sam finally looked up and saw a young marine standing over them. There were several other people gaping at them from farther down the corridor.

"We're fine, son, just fine," Sam said, getting up and lifting Eve to her feet.

"Uh, why were you two on the floor, sir?" the young man seemed compelled to ask.

"We fell in the aftershock," Sam explained, dusting off the skirt of Eve's gray wool suit.

Gray wool suit! What had happened to her green cocktail dress?

"What aftershock was that, sir?" the marine wanted to know.

Sam looked at Eve, who didn't seem as surprised as he felt. But, after all, she had been through this before. This was his first trip between universes.

"Don't worry, we'll get it right this time, sweetheart," they said in unison.

Chapter Fourteen

A half hour after the quake, the phone rang. Sitting at Sam's side on the living room couch, Eve reached across his body to get the telephone receiver. As she put it to her ear, Sam turned off the sound on the television using the remote-control device.

"Hello?"

"Eve? It's me, Janet. I'm calling from Lake Tahoe. Steve got here, too."

"Janet! Oh, thank God. I tried calling the lodge several times. At first they said neither of you had checked in, and then I couldn't get through at all. I was so worried that your lawyer didn't find you. Or that you had refused to go up there."

When it turned out they couldn't contact Steven until he returned from his business trip late on the thirtieth, Eve decided to set up the same ruse she had used in the last world. It was easier than trying to explain to Steven anything about their own trip— through the barriers of time and space. And it appeared to have worked.

"Are you all right, Janet?" Eve placed the phone so that Sam could hear the other end of the conversation. He took her free hand and laced his fingers with hers.

"Oh, yes, although Susan Cohn couldn't connect with me until late this morning," Janet was saying. "I tried calling you, but the long-distance lines were jammed. So I just drove up here. Eve, if you hadn't set up this portrait pretense, I probably would have been under a pile of rubble in that rat-trap apartment I'd rented. I was painting up a storm and didn't hear a thing about the earthquake warnings. Are you watching the first news reports coming in from Berkeley?"

"The television is on," Eve confirmed with a glance at the silent screen.

"Looks like there's lots of structural damage, but hardly anyone is hurt. They're calling that geologist from the university a hero. It must have taken a lot of courage for him to stick out his professional neck and make an official prediction yesterday morning. After that, there was nothing the authorities could do except evacuate the most dangerous buildings and close down the freeways. Sure looks like it helped."

"Yeah . . . this time it worked." Eve sighed, then grinned at Sam. They had done good!

After emerging into this universe at four in the afternoon of December 29th, they had driven right up to Berkeley and cornered Dave Sutter. This time they were armed with some potent ammunition, thanks to Eve's trick memory and Sam's love of the comic pages.

They used the information they had both garnered from reading the December 30th morning newspaper at Rubio's Pizzeria in their last world. Eve told Dave exactly what the scores would be for all the sporting events taking place on the twenty-ninth, and Sam outlined the "plots" of all the comic strips he had read at Rubio's.

Since some of those games were still in progress, or would take place that night, Eve and Sam had sat on pins and needles in Dave's house as the results came in, one by one.

Except for a hockey game—which had been very close in their previous universe—all of her predictions eventually proved correct.

The topper came early the next morning when Dave got his *Chronicle* and read the comic pages. Since Sam's descriptions matched in every detail, Dave was finally convinced that Eve and Sam really had jumped between parallel universes.

After that, using the data from his own experimental readings, which *did* indicate significant changes in the earth's magnetism around Berkeley, Dave issued his now famous prediction, at eleven, yesterday morning.

And that seemed to have made all the difference. It meant life instead of death or injury for thousands of people, including Hertha Jenkins's family. Having heard Dave's prediction, she and Joe were already packing the cars for the trip to Monterey, yesterday afternoon, when Sam finally tracked them down at their daughter's home in San Francisco.

"Eve, are you still there?" Janet's voice broke into her sister's satisfied thoughts.

"Oh, sorry. I was just thinking about all the people who have survived the quake. Janet, I hope you weren't angry that instead of a mystery friend who wanted his picture painted, you got..."

"Steve?" her sister finished for her. "I've never seen him like this. All apologetic and contrite—pleading that he's ready to get some professional help for his Don Juan syndrome. By the way, I can talk freely because he's out buying us some champagne. Steve probably didn't want to invest in a bottle if it was going to end up launching his head into orbit."

Janet's giggle was a sound Eve hadn't heard in way too long. Even if *this* woman was not her "birth" sister, or even the same person Eve had tried to contact in her second universe, it felt like she was talking to the original Janet.

Hopefully, her plot had worked as well in the last world she had visited. And Eve prayed that, back in her home universe, her real sister was safe. But she would never know. Damn, it was all so complicated!

"Eve...oh, Eve, can you ever forgive me?" The troubled voice of this world's Janet pulled Eve out of the twisting tangle of her multidimensional travels.

"Steve may have had a deep psychological problem to explain what he did last year," Janet went on. "But what can I say about myself...except that I was a jealous jerk."

"No, not a jerk. Janet, I won't say that I wasn't hurt and angered by what you and Steven did. I don't quite qualify for sainthood, yet. But I can understand what it must have been like to be compared to an older sibling all through school. And I probably wasn't as sensitive to your feelings back then as I should have been. I remember how much I resented having to tutor you, and missing out on being with my friends.

"And don't think that my relationship with our parents was so perfect...either." Eve smiled wryly at

Sam. "With some recent help, I finally realized that I was very unhappy with the way they pushed me... almost forcing me into a career in music I didn't want. So why don't we just say that we have a lot to talk about... that we'll both have to work on repairing our relationship?"

"Okay, Eve. I just hope you think I'm worth the effort."

"Of course, I do. Janet, remember when you said last year that you fell in love with Steven at first sight? I didn't believe you at the time, but now I do."

Eve looked up at Sam. She pointed to her eyes and her heart and then at him. As always, he got her drift, and nodded his agreement.

"You do? Well, I'm not so sure anymore. Look what it got me... a husband who chases anything in skirts."

"Honey... give him a chance. I finally figured out that he must love you very much. And everybody deserves a second chance."

"Including me, Eve?"

"Absolutely. However, I just got engaged... again. And there is no way I would ever forgive you if you came on to my Sam."

"You're engaged?" Janet shrieked through the phone. "Eve's engaged! Steve just came back. Tell me everything."

"At the next opportunity. Give me a call in a few days and we'll get together. I have this wedding to plan for next weekend, and I sure could use some help from my sister."

"You'll have it, Eve. I'll call on Tuesday."

Eve hung up the phone, and then turned to Sam. She just smiled at him for a long minute. Her Sam. Really hers.

When they found themselves in this universe, they had made a quick check of the situation here. They learned most things were similar to Sam's home base. It seemed they must not have traveled over as many universes this time, as Eve had on her first journey. Maybe, it was because there had been two of them this go-round.

Whatever the reason, the Sam native to this world was also a widower, having lost Amber on their honeymoon. And he had come to work at the Monterey facility earlier in the month.

As far as Eve's counterpart—she had lost her parents in the previous year, been jilted by Steven, and had put up a Christmas tree.

"I'm surprised that Jack Kennedy's assassination didn't cause more differences between this world and my own." Eve continued her comparison list out loud. She had spent an hour this morning going through a book from her counterpart's collection that had a timeline format. The volume listed the major events in world history and culture up to five years ago.

"Eve! Do you mean he wasn't shot in your home universe?"

"No. Was he in yours?"

Sam nodded.

"Oh, my! I wonder what else we'll find different from our home worlds when we really have time to check. Besides the fact that Mozart didn't write a forty-second symphony in this universe, either."

"Well, I have a suggestion about that one. Given your wonderful memory, why don't you write out the score you heard on the tape, and claim to have discovered a long, lost manuscript?" Sam offered with a wide grin.

"Sam, I'm surprised at you! Besides, it would never work." Eve laughed. "The paper I wrote it on wouldn't be old enough. But... but, it *could* be published as a work done in his style, and the proceeds would go to our favorite charities. Hey, think about all the good work Father Moreno could do with that windfall."

"Eve, I love that devious mind of yours."

"Thank you, thank you." She bowed her head at him in recognition of the teasing compliment. "We could have done the same thing with the Sarban sequel to *The Sound of His Horn.* I'm so sorry I never got more than a glimpse at the novel. Now it's lost to us forever because there's no way I'm going back to the facility tonight and take another magical mystery trip into some other universe!"

On the drive up to Berkeley on the twenty-ninth, in this time track, they had tried to figure out exactly what had happened to them. Their best guess was that the unique combination of the aftershock and some sort of energy leak into the corridor from the LinkUp test had sent them off into this newest world.

Although there might have been other factors involved. The sun was in a high sunspot mode right now, so perhaps an extra-powerful solar flare had contributed to the conditions.

Just what spatial perimeters were involved, they might never know. Unless they could convince the authorities there actually was a phenomenon associated with the usage of the LinkUp equipment.

"Eve, we forgot about that corridor!" Sam suddenly shouted. "What if someone wanders past the corner when they test the LinkUp experiment in..." He looked at his watch and then quickly grabbed Eve as the room shook with the midnight aftershock.

"In no seconds. Happy New Year, my love." Sam planted a long, deep kiss on her mouth. Afterward, they sat for several minutes, content to hold on to the magnificent riches they had in this world—each other.

"But you know, Eve," Sam's voice abruptly broke into the comfortable silence, "I never understood what you have against Mozart's fortieth."

"And you never will! I can't tell you how sorry I am for Sam One, and what I did to him because of my carelessness with that piece of music."

"Does that mean you and I never can listen to it together?" Sam asked softly. "Are you telling me I've lost the pleasure of sharing it with you?"

"Oh, no, darling. I'm sorry if that's how it sounded. Of course we can listen to it together. I'll just have to keep telling myself to keep my big mouth shut."

Shaking his head, Sam reached over to switch off the silent earthquake reports still flashing across the television screen. They would find out all they needed to know in the morning.

He then got up and went over to the tape deck, inserting a cassette into the player.

Coming back to stand in front of Eve, he listened to the opening bars of the fortieth symphony. Eve put her hand over her mouth and, with eyes full of mischief, pressed her lips firmly together.

"You know, when I was taking music appreciation in college," Sam mused, "my instructor gave us a way to remember this symphony. It went, 'Mozart's in the closet . . . let him out, let him out . . . let him out.'"

"Sam! That's it...that's the ditty. You already knew it. And he—Sam One—probably took the same class as you did and learned that jingle, too. Oh, that's wonderful. I had been feeling so bad about it. If you can imagine such a thing, considering all my other troubles." She laughed and jumped up to give him a hard kiss.

"Well, I'll just have to give you something better to associate this symphony with from now on." He took Eve's hand and led her toward the kitchen. "Come, love. While the music plays, let's have a good look at our new universe."

Outside, in the unusually warm January 1st night, they sat nestled in each others arms on the plump cushions of the sturdy redwood furniture. Leaning back, Sam and Eve watched bright stars, which were brand new to them, wheel in constellation patterns as old as human imagination.

When the full moon rose over the eucalyptus trees, and thousands of monarch butterfly wings stirred the air in age-old homage, Eve turned to Sam.

"Some things will never change, my darling. The stars, the moon...or my love for you." She raised the large, masculine hand clasped tightly in hers and kissed long, strong fingers one by one.

Sam captured her chin with his free hand and raised her face so that he could see the emotion in her moonstruck eyes. He also knew Eve could see the same thing in his own irises...living mirrors reflecting infinite love.

"We were destined for each other in an endless number of worlds, my love. And I swear to you that we will never be apart in this one, until the day we die."

The heat of Sam's searing kiss generated a cocoon of warmth around them so intense that when he opened her blouse to nuzzle her breasts, Eve felt no chill. And the radiance only became greater as each explored the other, learning the new and exalting in the familiar.

"Sam!" Eve finally implored an eternity later, communicating with that one word her readiness for his possession.

"Come with me, my own dearest heart," Sam called to her in response. "Join me at the end of the universe."

"I'm there with you, my darling Sam. At the end of this universe and what others there may be!"

And out there, in that bright unknown, the essence that was the best of Sam and Eve merged to form the unique soul...who in nine months' time would be their first-born child.

A HOLIDAY RECIPE FROM THE KITCHEN OF

Phyllis Houseman

Here's a recipe you may remember from the book. It's a family tradition at our house! Enjoy!

JULIE'S POTATO LATKES

6 large potatoes, peeled
1 medium onion
8 slices white bread, torn into small pieces and soaked in 1 cup water
1/2 tsp pepper
1/4 cup cooking oil

Grate potatoes and onion in a large bowl (or you can use a food processor). Squeeze the water out of the bread and add to potato/onion mixture. Add pepper and mix well.

In a large skillet heat the oil to medium high (375° F). Drop heaping tablespoons of mixture into hot oil and press down with a spoon. Cook 3-5 minutes, until browned, then turn and cook on the other side until browned.

Serve with sour cream and/or applesauce.

HARLEQUIN®

AMERICAN ◆ ROMANCE®

It happened in an instant, but it would last a lifetime.

Suddenly

For three unlikely couples, courtship with kids is anything but slow and easy. Meet the whole brood as three popular American Romance authors show you how much fun it can be in a "family affair"!

#647 CHASING BABY
by Pam McCutcheon
September 1996

#655 MARRYING NICKIE
by Vivian Leiber
November 1996

#664 ROMANCING ANNIE
by Nikki Rivers
January 1997

a Family

Look us up on-line at: http://www.romance.net

SAF

HARLEQUIN®
AMERICAN ◆ ROMANCE®

The Randall Brothers—living out there on their Wyoming ranch with only each other, their ranch hands and the cattle for company.... Well, it could make a body yearn for female companionship! Much as they miss womenfolk, these four cowboys don't cotton to being roped and branded in matrimony! But then big brother Jake brings home four of the most beautiful "fillies."

Don't miss what happens next to

Chad—COWBOY CUPID October '96

Pete—COWBOY DADDY November '96

Brett—COWBOY GROOM January '97

Jake—COWBOY SURRENDER February '97

4 Brides
for 4 Brothers

They give new meaning to the term "gettin' hitched"!

1997
Reader's Engagement Book
A calendar of important dates
and anniversaries for readers to use!

Informative and entertaining—with notable
dates and trivia highlighted throughout the year.

Handy, convenient, pocketbook size to help you
keep track of your own personal important dates.

Added bonus—contains $5.00 worth of coupons
for upcoming Harlequin and Silhouette books.
This calendar more than pays for itself!

Available beginning in November at
your favorite retail outlet.

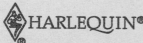

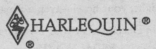